W9-BZT-183

31668074235331

DISNEY

FROZEN

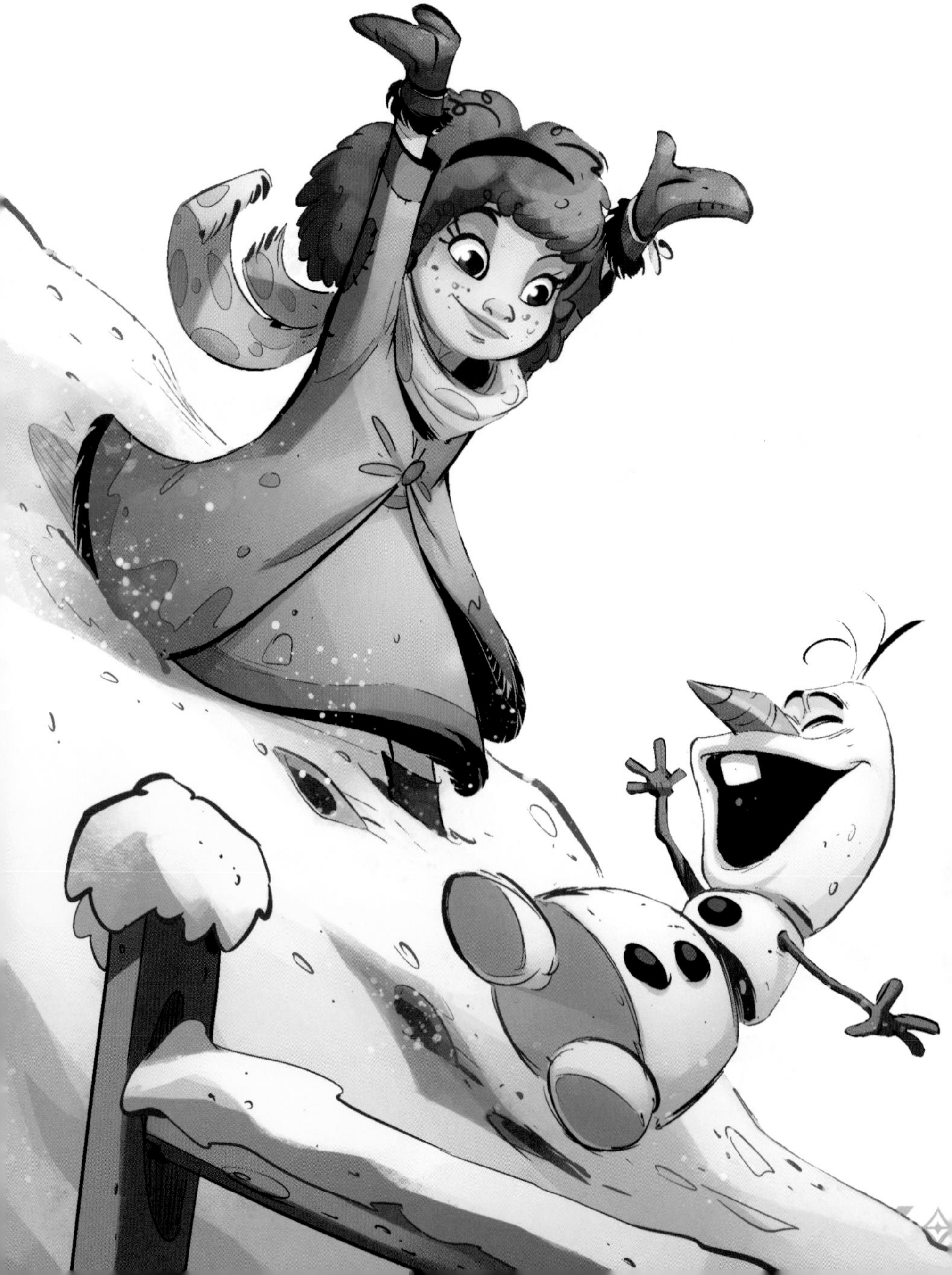

THE HERO WITHIN

STORY & SCRIPT BY
JOE CARAMAGNA

ART BY
KAWAII CREATIVE STUDIOS

LETTERING BY
**RICHARD STARKINGS
& COMICRAFT'S JIMMY BETANCOURT**

COVER ART BY
KAWAII CREATIVE STUDIOS

DARK HORSE BOOKS

DARK HORSE BOOKS

PRESIDENT AND PUBLISHER
MIKE RICHARDSON

EDITOR
FREDDYE MILLER

DESIGNER
SKYLER WEISSENFLUH

ASSISTANT EDITOR
JUDY KHUU

DIGITAL ART TECHNICIAN
SAMANTHA HUMMER

Neil Hankerson Executive Vice President • **Tom Weddle** Chief Financial Officer • **Randy Stradley** Vice President of Publishing • **Nick McWhorter** Chief Business Development Officer • **Dale LaFountain** Chief Information Officer • **Matt Parkinson** Vice President of Marketing • **Cara Niece** Vice President of Production and Scheduling • **Mark Bernardi** Vice President of Book Trade and Digital Sales • **Ken Lizzi** General Counsel • **Dave Marshall** Editor in Chief • **Davey Estrada** Editorial Director • **Chris Warner** Senior Books Editor • **Cary Grazzini** Director of Specialty Projects • **Lia Ribacchi** Art Director • **Vanessa Todd-Holmes** Director of Print Purchasing • **Matt Dryer** Director of Digital Art and Prepress • **Michael Gombos** Senior Director of Licensed Publications • **Kari Yadro** Director of Custom Programs • **Kari Torson** Director of International Licensing • **Sean Brice** Director of Trade Sales

DISNEY PUBLISHING WORLDWIDE GLOBAL MAGAZINES, COMICS AND PARTWORKS

PUBLISHER Lynn Waggoner • EDITORIAL TEAM Bianca Coletti (Director, Magazines), Guido Frazzini (Director, Comics), Carlotta Quattrocolo (Executive Editor), Stefano Ambrosio (Executive Editor, New IP), Camilla Vedove (Senior Manager, Editorial Development), Behnoosh Khalili (Senior Editor), Julie Dorris (Senior Editor), Mina Riazi (Assistant Editor) • DESIGN Enrico Soave (Senior Designer) • ART Ken Shue (VP, Global Art), Manny Mederos (Senior Illustration Manager, Comics and Magazines), Roberto Santillo (Creative Director), Marco Ghiglione (Creative Manager), Stefano Attardi (Illustration Manager) • PORTFOLIO MANAGEMENT Olivia Ciancarelli (Director) • BUSINESS & MARKETING Mariantonietta Galla (Senior Manager, Franchise), Virpi Korhonen (Editorial Manager)

DISNEY FROZEN: THE HERO WITHIN
Frozen © 2019 Disney Enterprises, Inc. All Rights Reserved. Dark Horse Books® and the Dark Horse logo are registered trademarks of Dark Horse Comics LLC. All rights reserved. No portion of this publication may be reproduced or transmitted, in any form or by any means, without the express written permission of Dark Horse Comics LLC. Names, characters, places, and incidents featured in this publication either are the product of the author's imagination or are used fictitiously. Any resemblance to actual persons (living or dead), events, institutions, or locales, without satiric intent, is coincidental.

Published by Dark Horse Books
A division of Dark Horse Comics LLC
10956 SE Main Street
Milwaukie, OR 97222

Darkhorse.com

To find a comics shop in your area, visit comicshoplocator.com

First edition: November 2019
ISBN 978-1-50671-269-7
Digital ISBN 978-1-50671-286-4

1 3 5 7 9 10 8 6 4 2
Printed in Canada

WELCOME TO ARENDELLE!

ELSA

The queen of the kingdom of Arendelle and Anna's older sister. Elsa has the ability to create snow and ice. She is confident, composed, creative, and warmhearted.

ANNA

The princess of Arendelle and Elsa's younger sister. Anna has faith in others and puts a positive spin on every situation. She is compassionate, fearless, and doesn't shy away from following her heart—no matter what.

OLAF

A snowman that Elsa brought to life. Olaf is a friend to all! He likes warm hugs and he is full of wonder and optimism—nothing can bring him down.

KRISTOFF

An ice harvester and the official ice master and deliverer of Arendelle. Raised by trolls in the mountains, he understands the importance of friends, family, and being true to yourself. He lives with his reindeer Sven.

SVEN

A reindeer and loyal best friend to Kristoff. They have regular conversations, and though Sven cannot communicate in words, sometimes Kristoff speaks for him. He enjoys carrots and lichen.

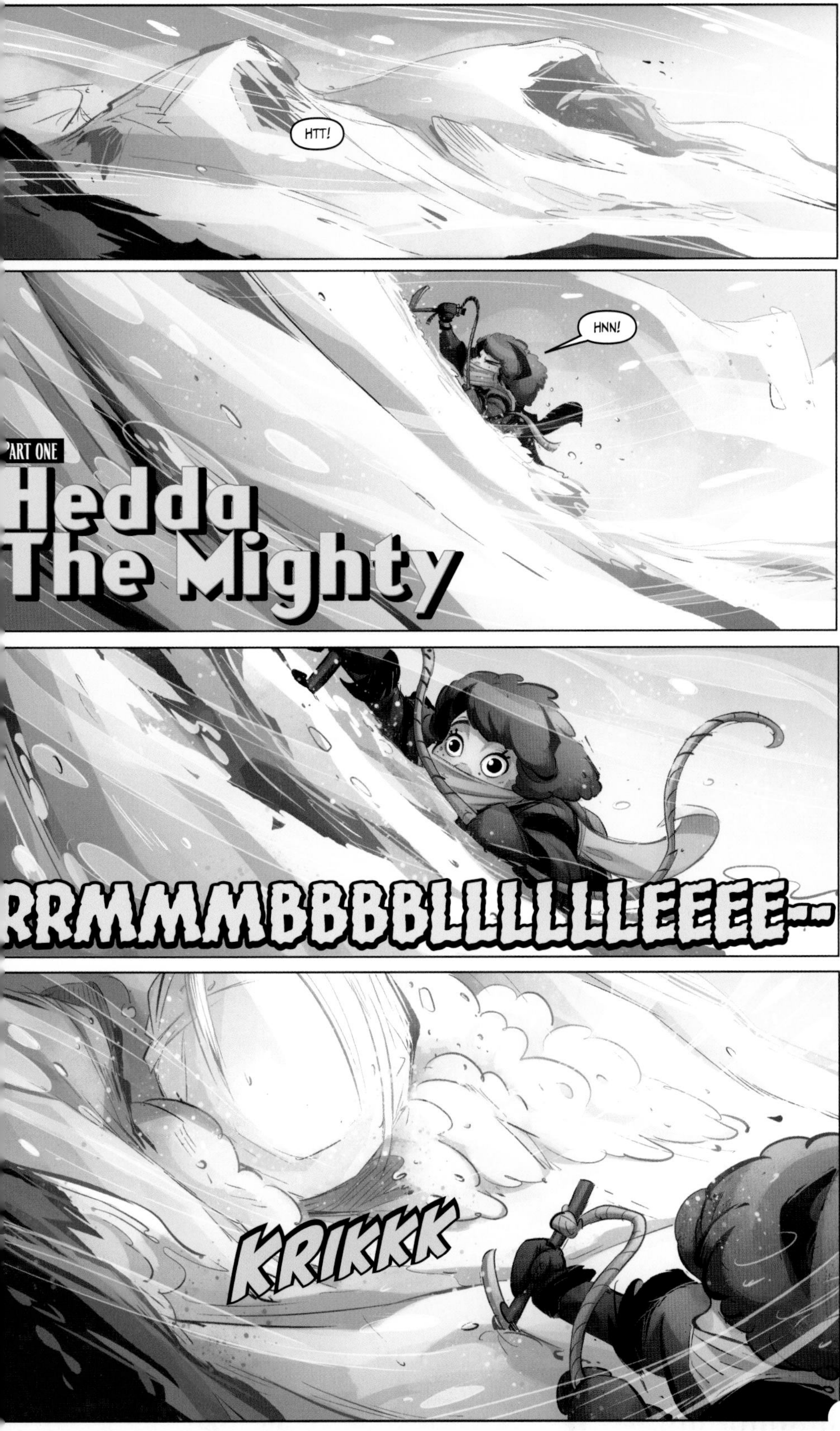
HTT!
HNN!
PART ONE
Hedda The Mighty
RRMMMBBBBLLLLLLLEEEE--
KRIKKK

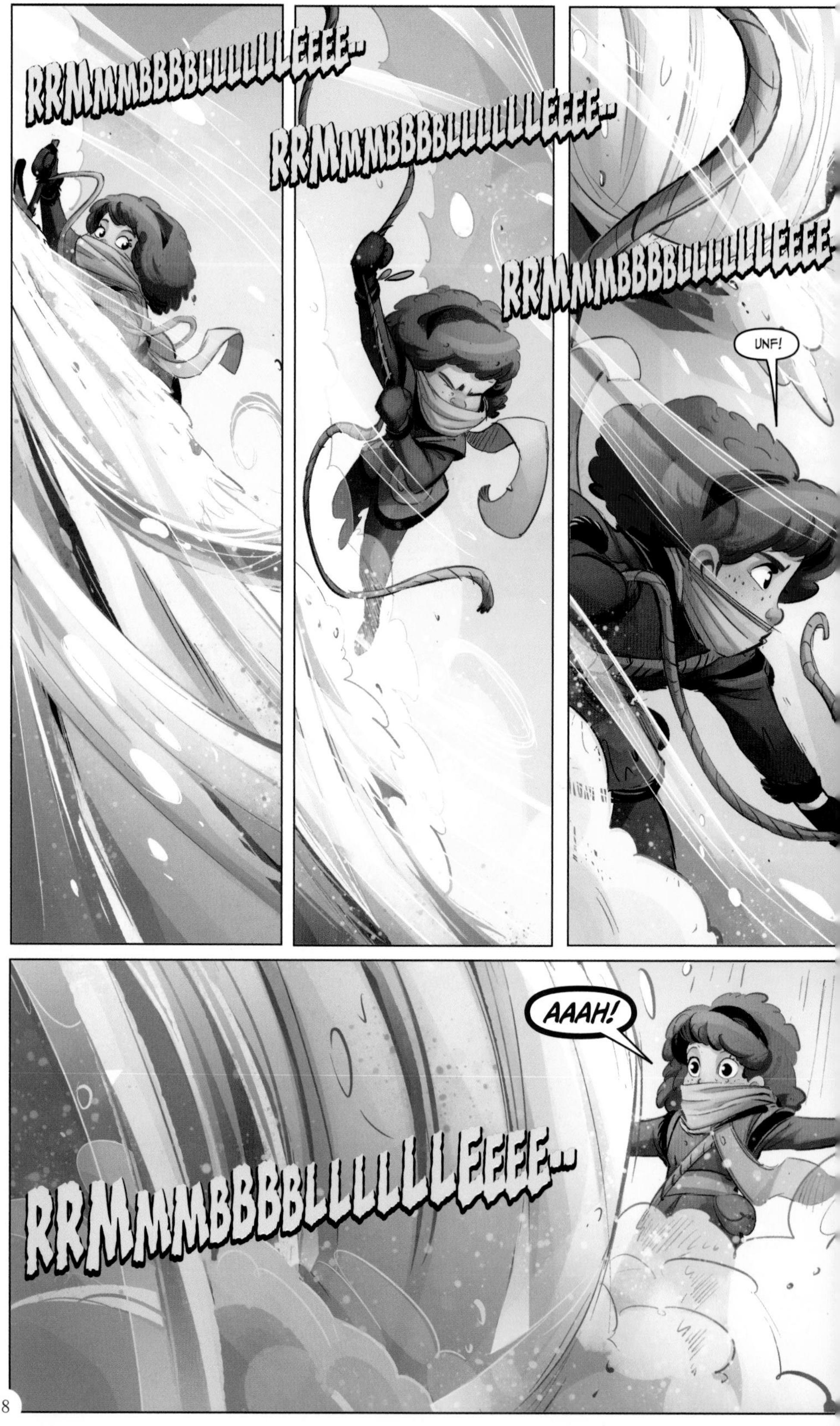
RRMMMBBBLLLLLLEEEE..
RRMMMBBBLLLLLLEEEE..
RRMMMBBBLLLLLLEEEE
UNF!
AAAH!
RRMMMBBBLLLLLLEEEE..

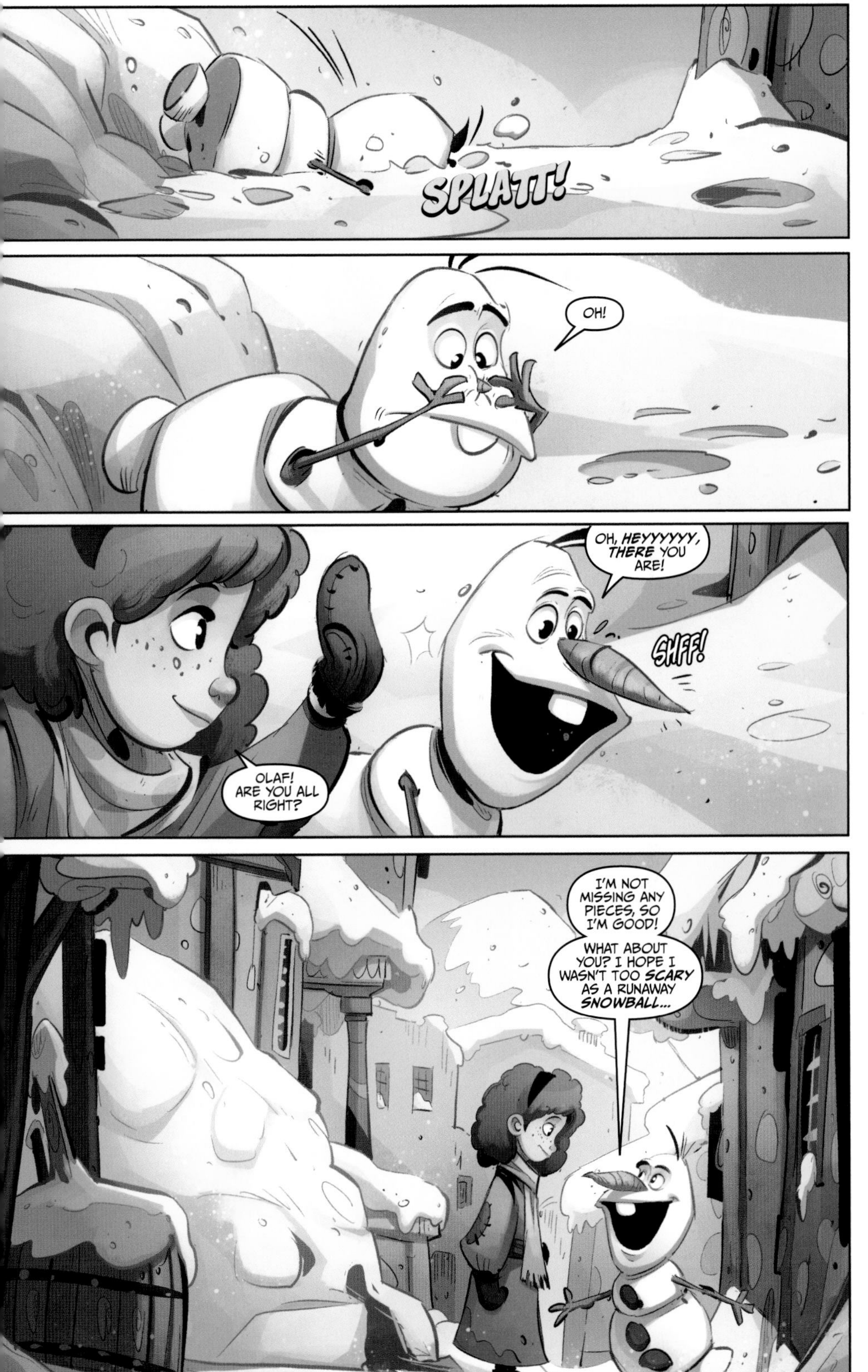
SPLATT!
OH!
OH, HEYYYYYY, THERE YOU ARE!
SHFF!
OLAF! ARE YOU ALL RIGHT?
I'M NOT MISSING ANY PIECES, SO I'M GOOD!
WHAT ABOUT YOU? I HOPE I WASN'T TOO SCARY AS A RUNAWAY SNOWBALL...

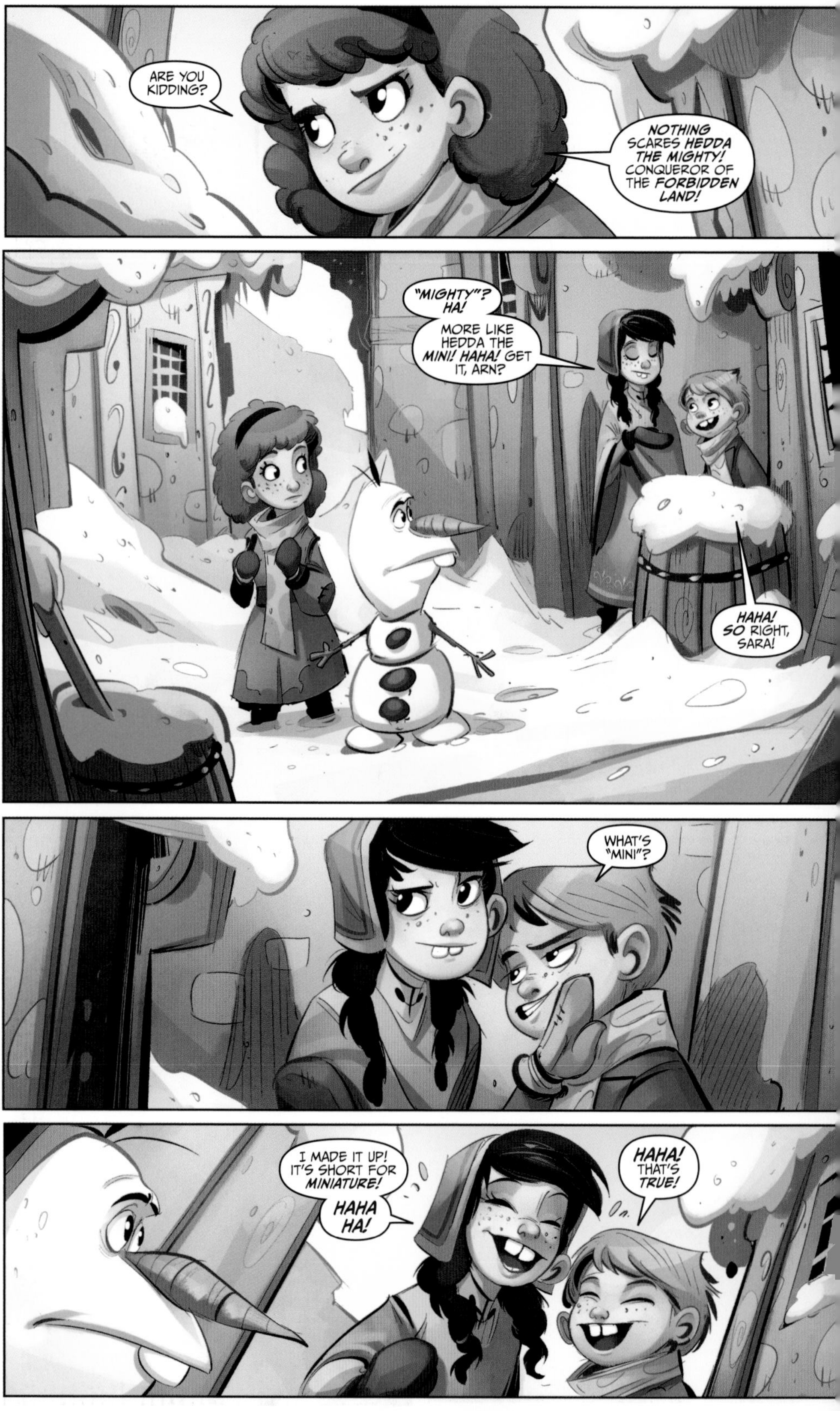

ARE YOU KIDDING?
NOTHING SCARES HEDDA THE MIGHTY! CONQUEROR OF THE FORBIDDEN LAND!
"MIGHTY"? HA!
MORE LIKE HEDDA THE MINI! HAHA! GET IT, ARN?
HAHA! SO RIGHT, SARA!
WHAT'S "MINI"?
I MADE IT UP! IT'S SHORT FOR MINIATURE!
HAHA HA!
HAHA! THAT'S TRUE!

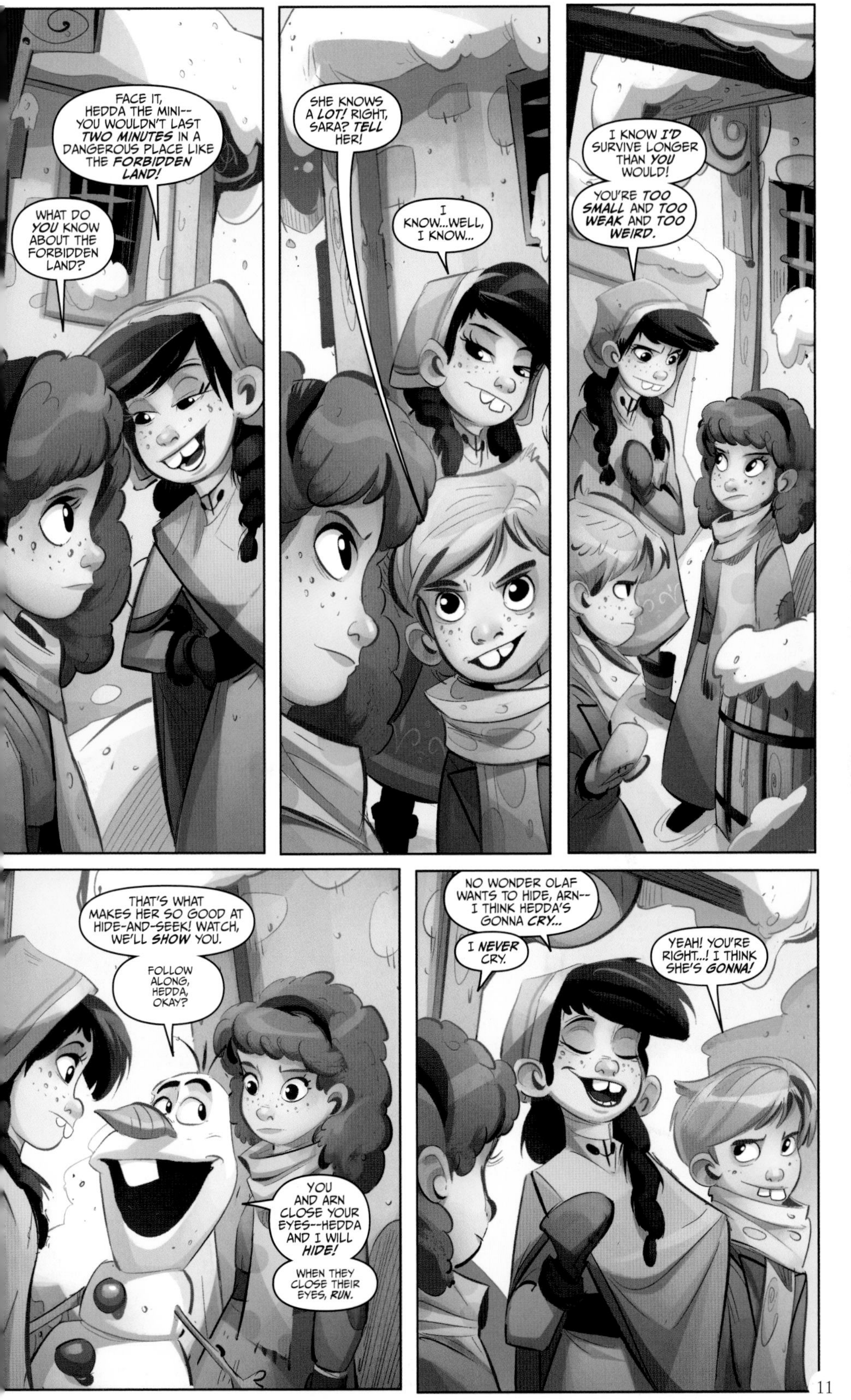

FACE IT, HEDDA THE MINI-- YOU WOULDN'T LAST TWO MINUTES IN A DANGEROUS PLACE LIKE THE FORBIDDEN LAND!
WHAT DO YOU KNOW ABOUT THE FORBIDDEN LAND?
SHE KNOWS A LOT! RIGHT, SARA? TELL HER!
I KNOW...WELL, I KNOW...
I KNOW I'D SURVIVE LONGER THAN YOU WOULD!
YOU'RE TOO SMALL AND TOO WEAK AND TOO WEIRD.
THAT'S WHAT MAKES HER SO GOOD AT HIDE-AND-SEEK! WATCH, WE'LL SHOW YOU.
FOLLOW ALONG, HEDDA, OKAY?
YOU AND ARN CLOSE YOUR EYES--HEDDA AND I WILL HIDE!
WHEN THEY CLOSE THEIR EYES, RUN.
NO WONDER OLAF WANTS TO HIDE, ARN-- I THINK HEDDA'S GONNA CRY...
I NEVER CRY.
YEAH! YOU'RE RIGHT...! I THINK SHE'S GONNA!

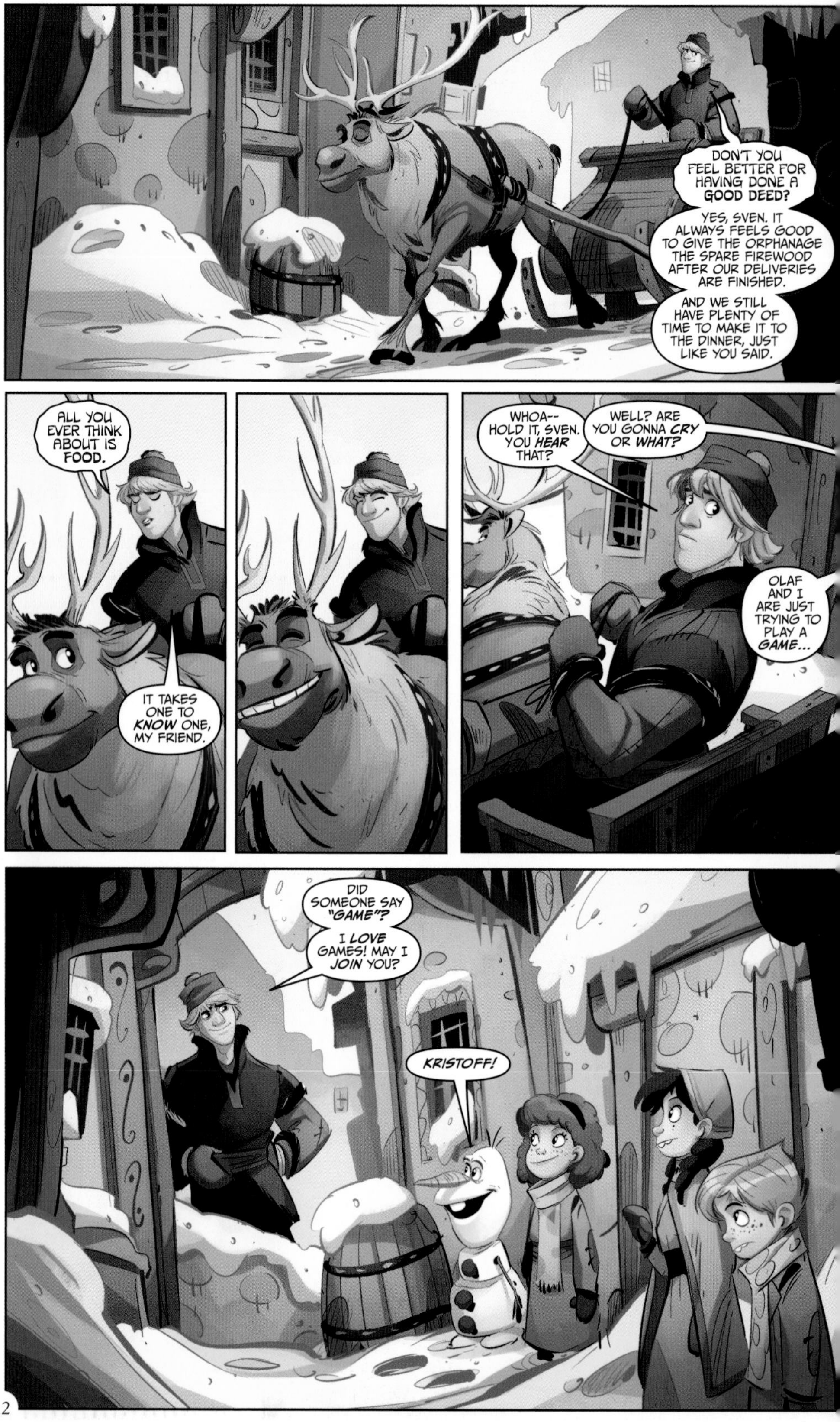
DON'T YOU FEEL BETTER FOR HAVING DONE A GOOD DEED?
YES, SVEN. IT ALWAYS FEELS GOOD TO GIVE THE ORPHANAGE THE SPARE FIREWOOD AFTER OUR DELIVERIES ARE FINISHED.
AND WE STILL HAVE PLENTY OF TIME TO MAKE IT TO THE DINNER, JUST LIKE YOU SAID.
ALL YOU EVER THINK ABOUT IS FOOD.
IT TAKES ONE TO KNOW ONE, MY FRIEND.
WELL? ARE YOU GONNA CRY OR WHAT?
WHOA-- HOLD IT, SVEN. YOU HEAR THAT?
OLAF AND I ARE JUST TRYING TO PLAY A GAME...
DID SOMEONE SAY "GAME"?
I LOVE GAMES! MAY I JOIN YOU?
KRISTOFF!

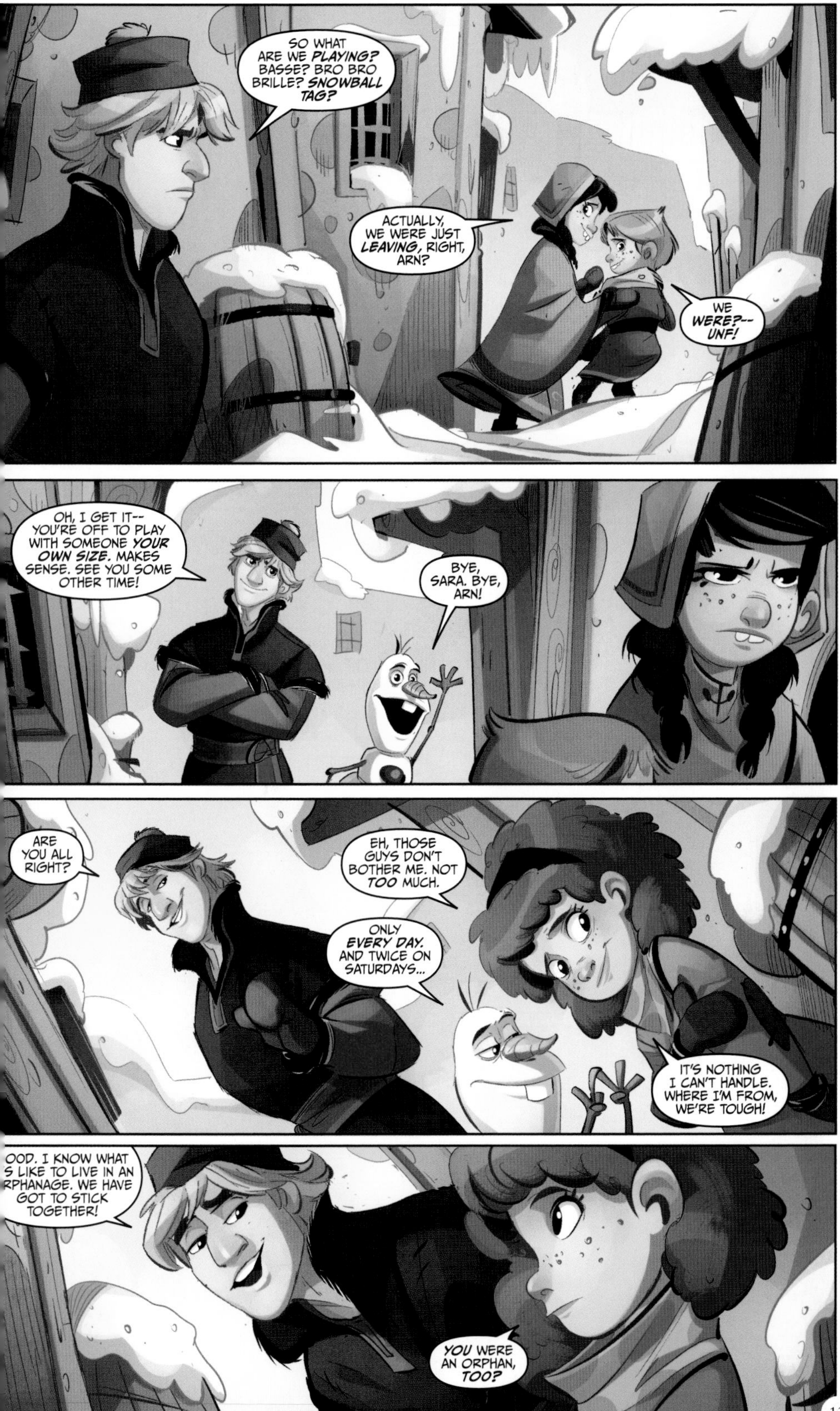
SO WHAT ARE WE PLAYING? BASSE? BRO BRO BRILLE? SNOWBALL TAG?
ACTUALLY, WE WERE JUST LEAVING, RIGHT, ARN?
WE WERE?-- UNF!
OH, I GET IT-- YOU'RE OFF TO PLAY WITH SOMEONE YOUR OWN SIZE. MAKES SENSE. SEE YOU SOME OTHER TIME!
BYE, SARA. BYE, ARN!
ARE YOU ALL RIGHT?
EH, THOSE GUYS DON'T BOTHER ME. NOT TOO MUCH.
ONLY EVERY DAY. AND TWICE ON SATURDAYS...
IT'S NOTHING I CAN'T HANDLE. WHERE I'M FROM, WE'RE TOUGH!
OOD. I KNOW WHAT S LIKE TO LIVE IN AN RPHANAGE. WE HAVE GOT TO STICK TOGETHER!
YOU WERE AN ORPHAN, TOO?

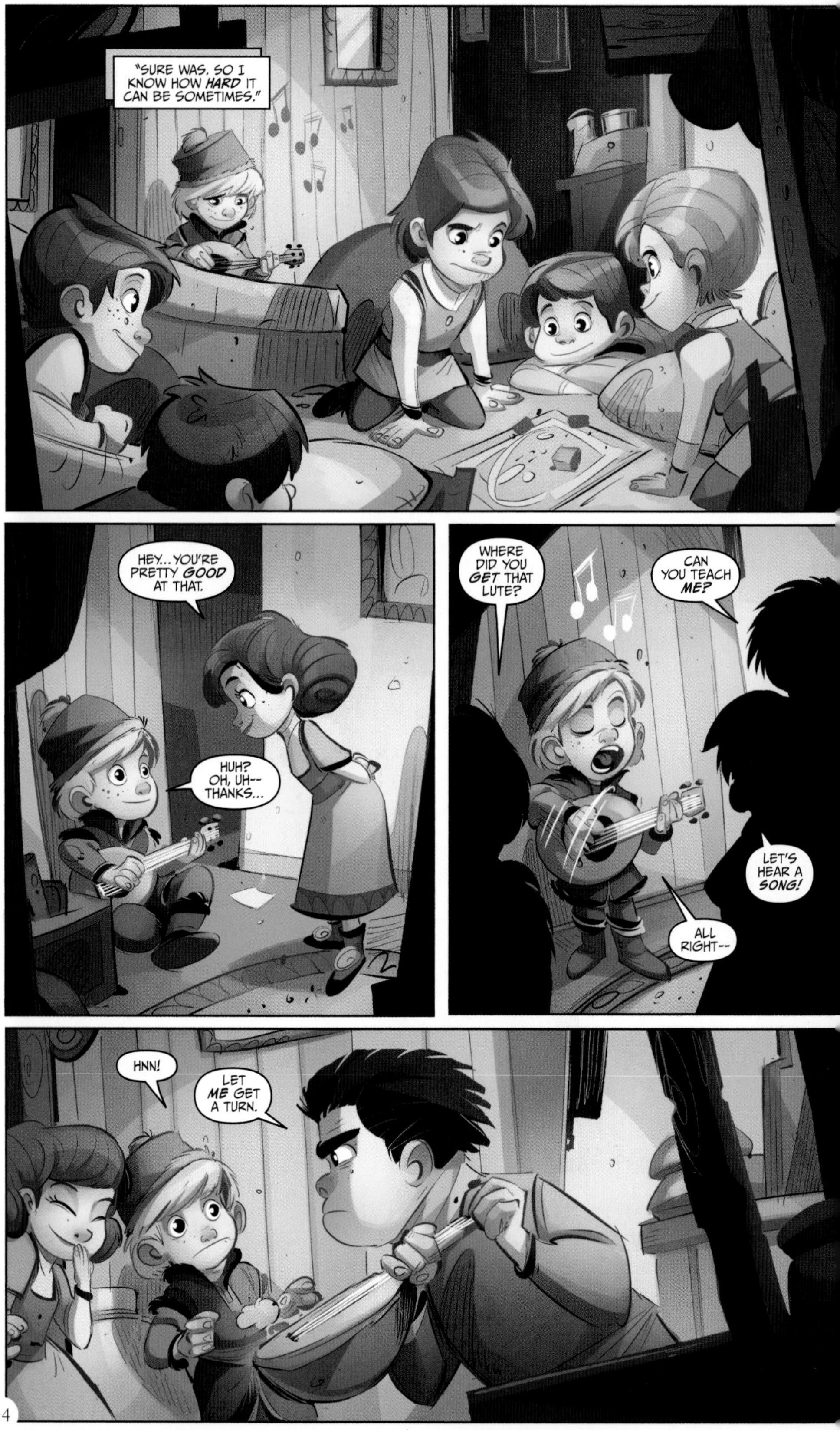
"SURE WAS. SO I KNOW HOW HARD IT CAN BE SOMETIMES."
HEY... YOU'RE PRETTY GOOD AT THAT.
HUH? OH, UH-- THANKS...
WHERE DID YOU GET THAT LUTE?
CAN YOU TEACH ME?
LET'S HEAR A SONG!
ALL RIGHT--
HNN!
LET ME GET A TURN.

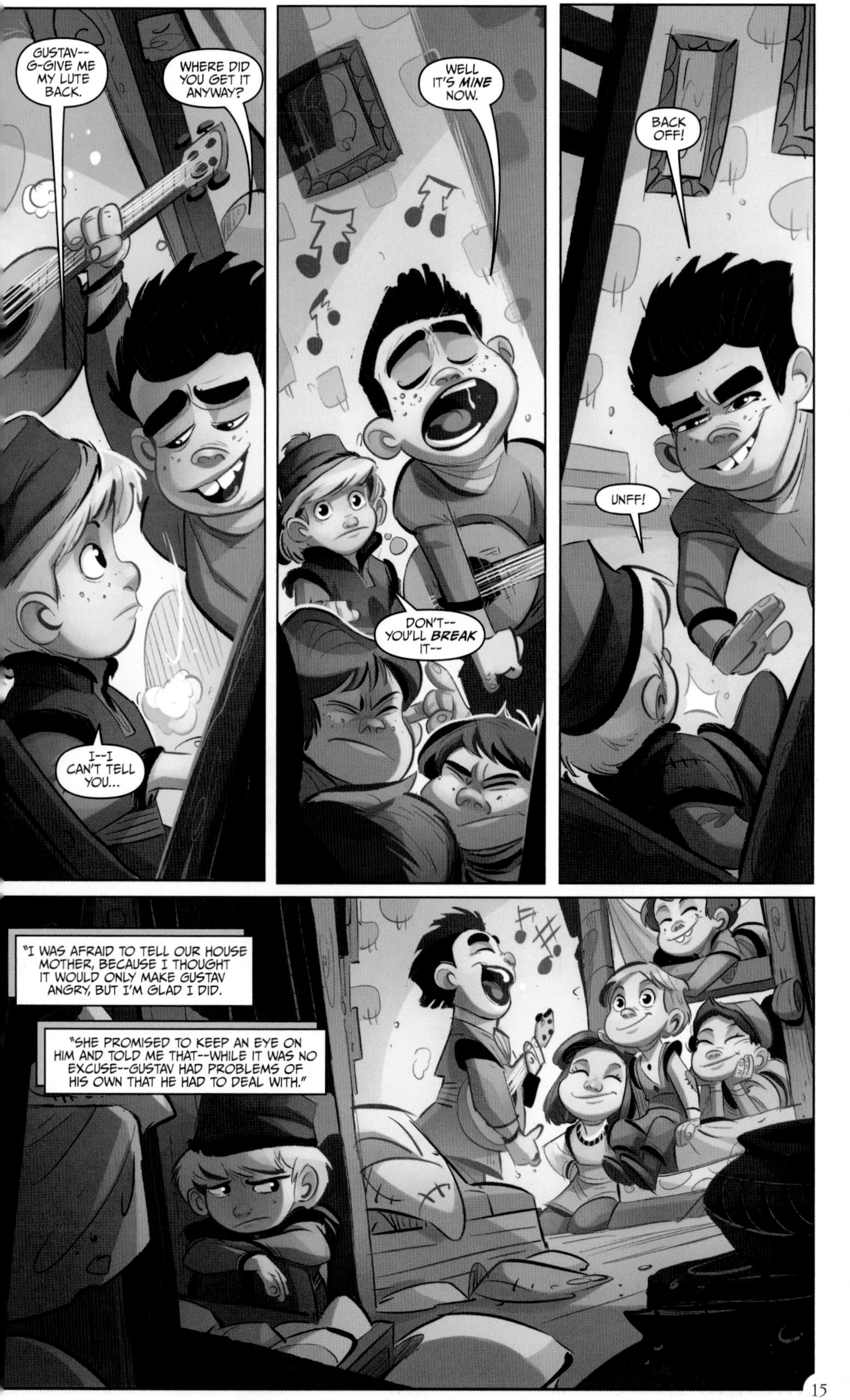

GUSTAV--
G-GIVE ME
MY LUTE
BACK.
WHERE DID
YOU GET IT
ANYWAY?
I--I
CAN'T TELL
YOU...
WELL
IT'S *MINE*
NOW.
DON'T--
YOU'LL *BREAK*
IT--
BACK
OFF!
UNFF!
"I WAS AFRAID TO TELL OUR HOUSE
MOTHER, BECAUSE I THOUGHT
IT WOULD ONLY MAKE GUSTAV
ANGRY, BUT I'M GLAD I DID.
"SHE PROMISED TO KEEP AN EYE ON
HIM AND TOLD ME THAT--WHILE IT WAS NO
EXCUSE--GUSTAV HAD PROBLEMS OF
HIS OWN THAT HE HAD TO DEAL WITH."

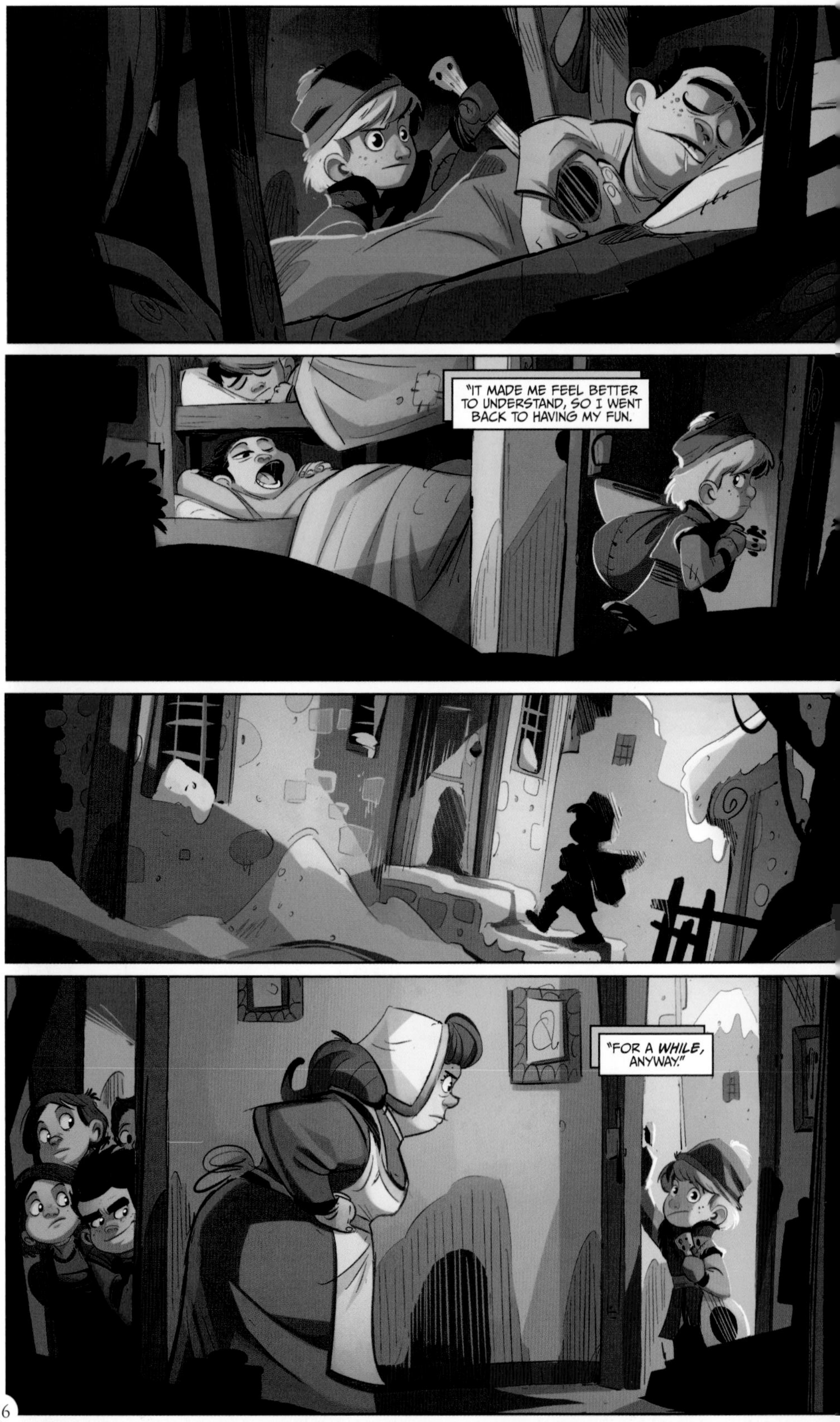
"IT MADE ME FEEL BETTER TO UNDERSTAND, SO I WENT BACK TO HAVING MY FUN.
"FOR A *WHILE*, ANYWAY."

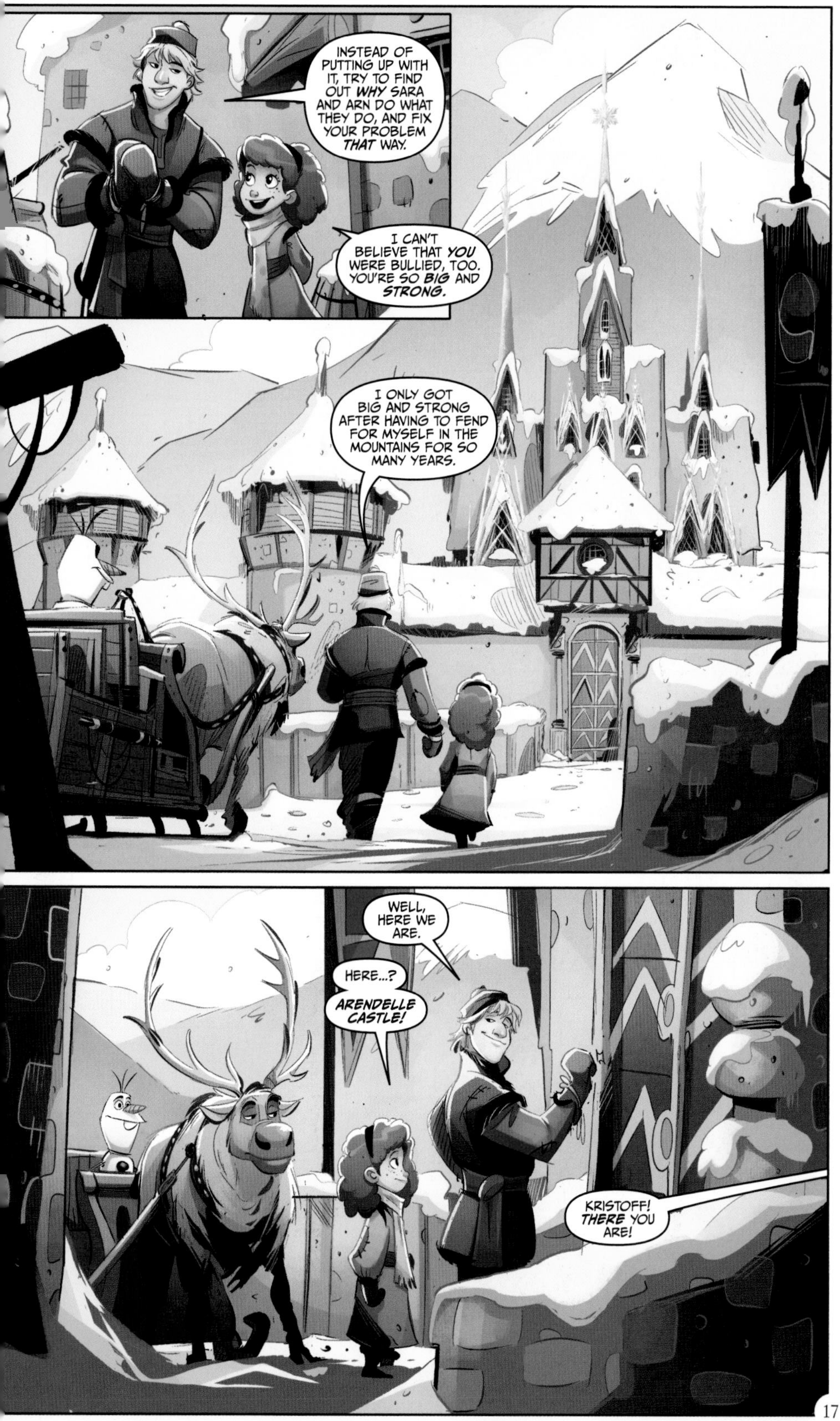
INSTEAD OF PUTTING UP WITH IT, TRY TO FIND OUT WHY SARA AND ARN DO WHAT THEY DO, AND FIX YOUR PROBLEM THAT WAY.
I CAN'T BELIEVE THAT YOU WERE BULLIED, TOO. YOU'RE SO BIG AND STRONG.
I ONLY GOT BIG AND STRONG AFTER HAVING TO FEND FOR MYSELF IN THE MOUNTAINS FOR SO MANY YEARS.
WELL, HERE WE ARE.
HERE...?
ARENDELLE CASTLE!
KRISTOFF! THERE YOU ARE!

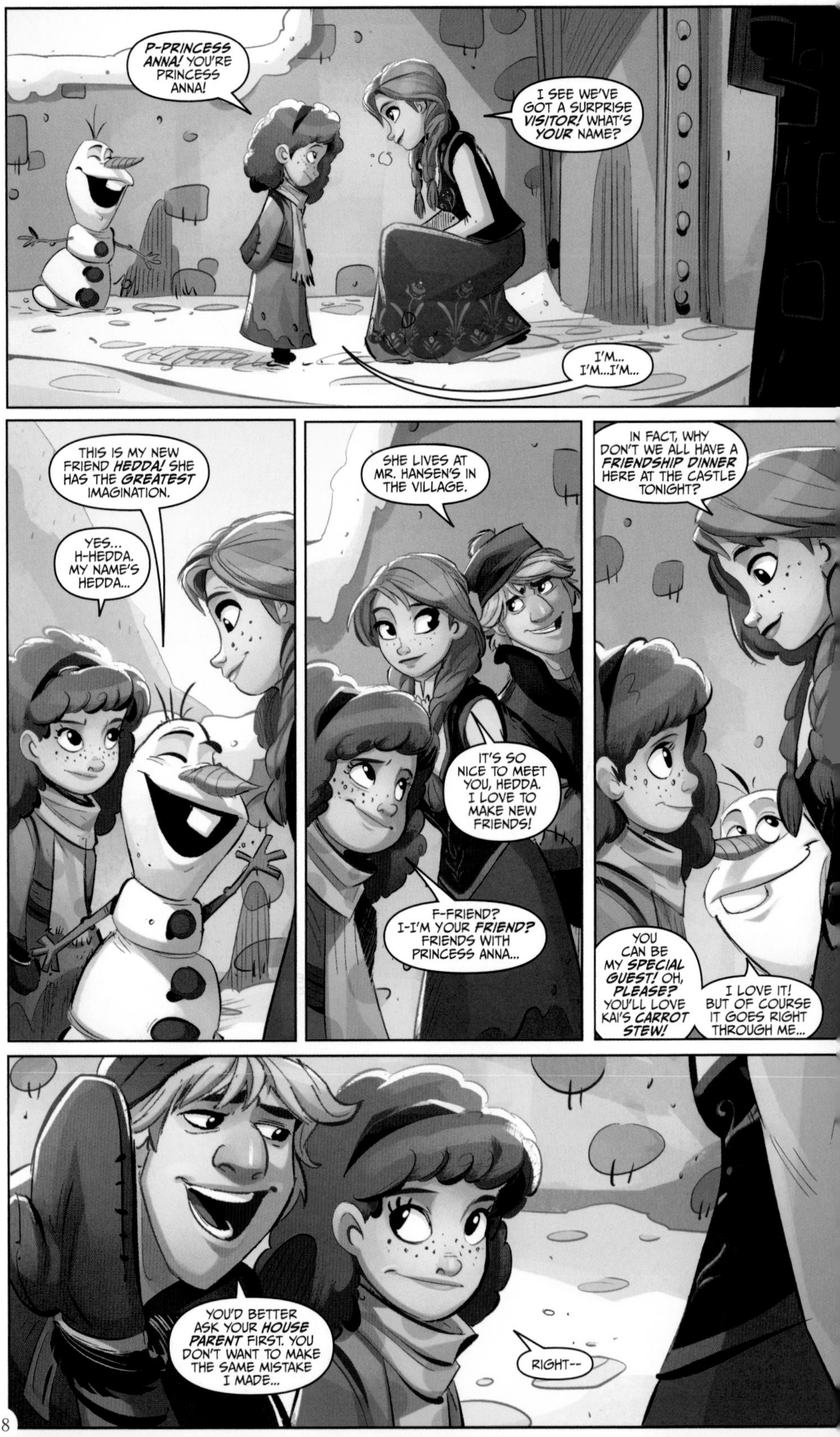
P-PRINCESS ANNA! YOU'RE PRINCESS ANNA!
I SEE WE'VE GOT A SURPRISE VISITOR! WHAT'S YOUR NAME?
I'M... I'M...I'M...
THIS IS MY NEW FRIEND HEDDA! SHE HAS THE GREATEST IMAGINATION.
YES... H-HEDDA. MY NAME'S HEDDA...
SHE LIVES AT MR. HANSEN'S IN THE VILLAGE.
IT'S SO NICE TO MEET YOU, HEDDA. I LOVE TO MAKE NEW FRIENDS!
F-FRIEND? I-I'M YOUR FRIEND? FRIENDS WITH PRINCESS ANNA...
IN FACT, WHY DON'T WE ALL HAVE A FRIENDSHIP DINNER HERE AT THE CASTLE TONIGHT?
YOU CAN BE MY SPECIAL GUEST! OH, PLEASE? YOU'LL LOVE KAI'S CARROT STEW!
I LOVE IT! BUT OF COURSE IT GOES RIGHT THROUGH ME...
YOU'D BETTER ASK YOUR HOUSE PARENT FIRST. YOU DON'T WANT TO MAKE THE SAME MISTAKE I MADE...
RIGHT--

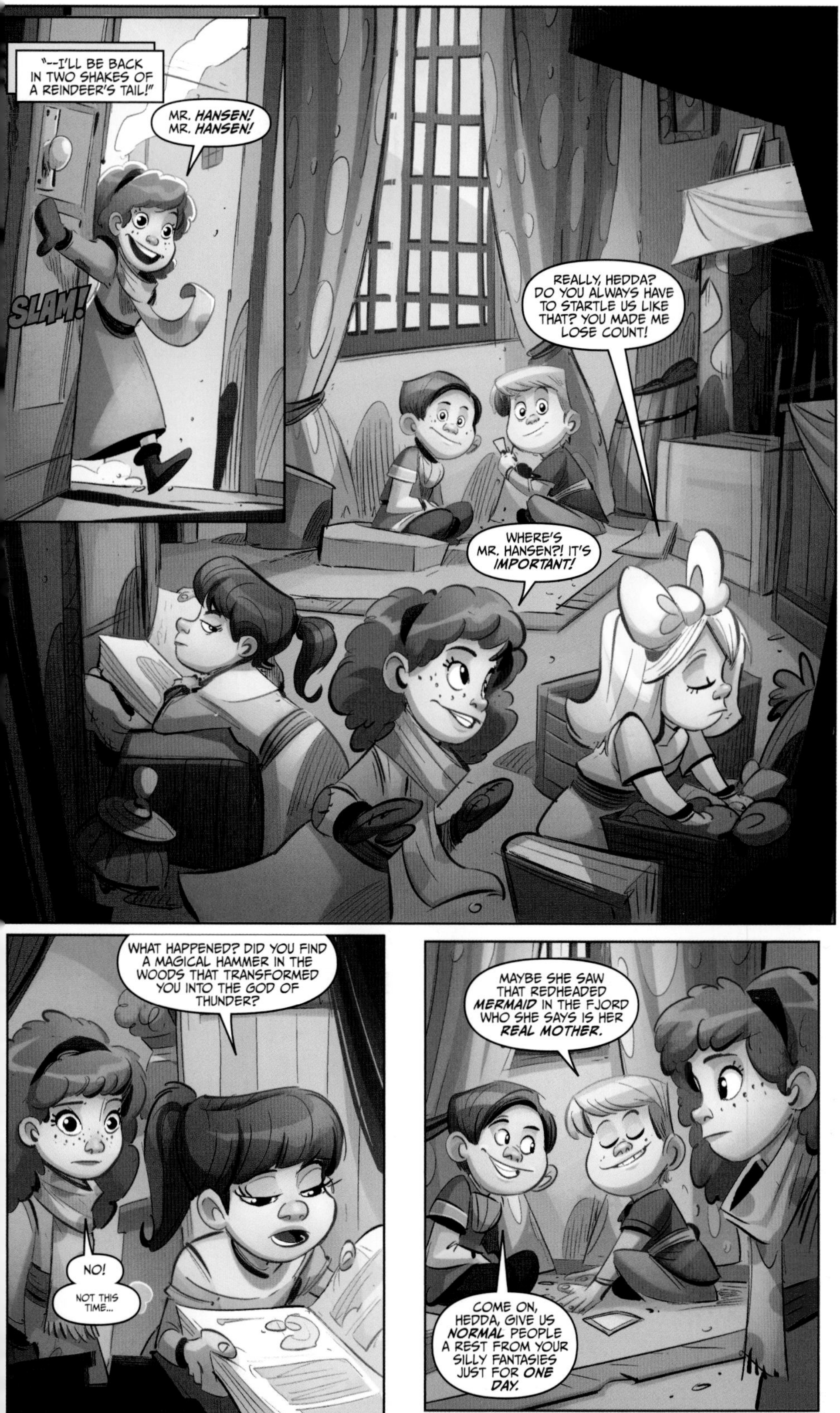
"--I'LL BE BACK IN TWO SHAKES OF A REINDEER'S TAIL!"
MR. HANSEN! MR. HANSEN!
SLAM!
REALLY, HEDDA? DO YOU ALWAYS HAVE TO STARTLE US LIKE THAT? YOU MADE ME LOSE COUNT!
WHERE'S MR. HANSEN?! IT'S IMPORTANT!
WHAT HAPPENED? DID YOU FIND A MAGICAL HAMMER IN THE WOODS THAT TRANSFORMED YOU INTO THE GOD OF THUNDER?
NO!
NOT THIS TIME...
MAYBE SHE SAW THAT REDHEADED MERMAID IN THE FJORD WHO SHE SAYS IS HER REAL MOTHER.
COME ON, HEDDA, GIVE US NORMAL PEOPLE A REST FROM YOUR SILLY FANTASIES JUST FOR ONE DAY.

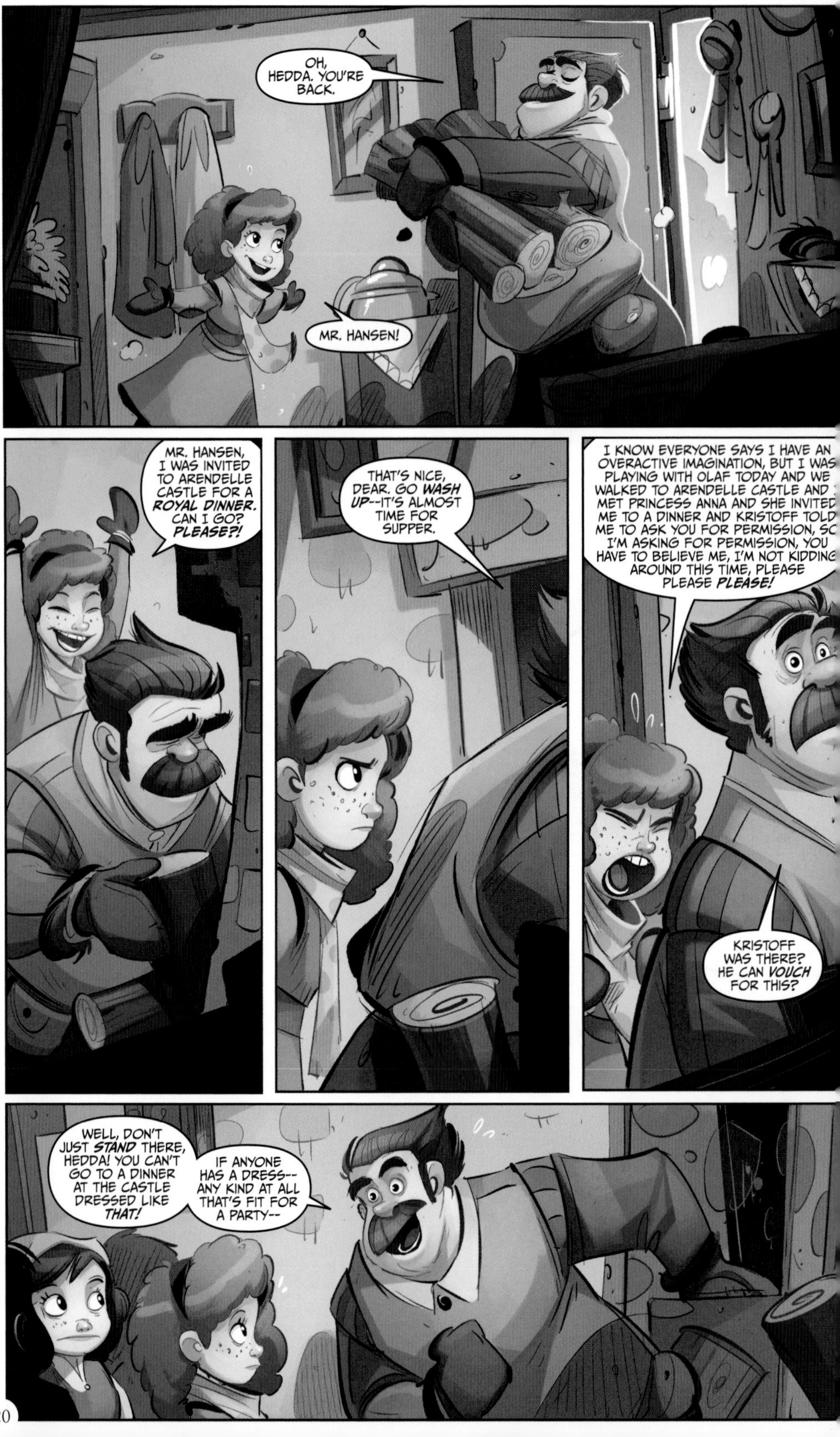

OH, HEDDA. YOU'RE BACK.
MR. HANSEN!
MR. HANSEN, I WAS INVITED TO ARENDELLE CASTLE FOR A ROYAL DINNER. CAN I GO? PLEASE?!
THAT'S NICE, DEAR. GO WASH UP--IT'S ALMOST TIME FOR SUPPER.
I KNOW EVERYONE SAYS I HAVE AN OVERACTIVE IMAGINATION, BUT I WAS PLAYING WITH OLAF TODAY AND WE WALKED TO ARENDELLE CASTLE AND I MET PRINCESS ANNA AND SHE INVITED ME TO A DINNER AND KRISTOFF TOLD ME TO ASK YOU FOR PERMISSION, SO I'M ASKING FOR PERMISSION, YOU HAVE TO BELIEVE ME, I'M NOT KIDDING AROUND THIS TIME, PLEASE PLEASE PLEASE!
KRISTOFF WAS THERE? HE CAN VOUCH FOR THIS?
WELL, DON'T JUST STAND THERE, HEDDA! YOU CAN'T GO TO A DINNER AT THE CASTLE DRESSED LIKE THAT!
IF ANYONE HAS A DRESS-- ANY KIND AT ALL THAT'S FIT FOR A PARTY--

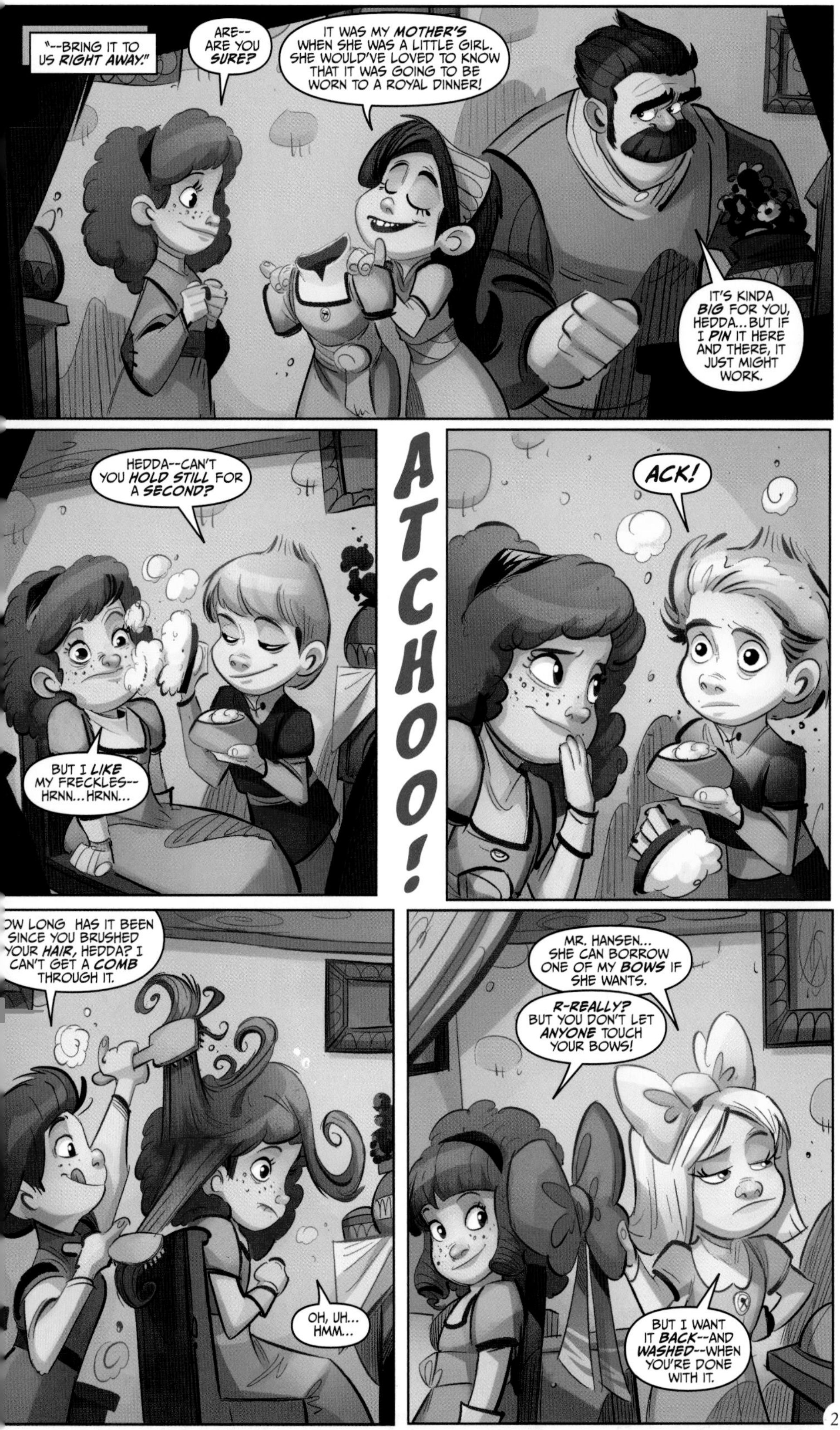

"--BRING IT TO US RIGHT AWAY."
ARE-- ARE YOU SURE?
IT WAS MY MOTHER'S WHEN SHE WAS A LITTLE GIRL. SHE WOULD'VE LOVED TO KNOW THAT IT WAS GOING TO BE WORN TO A ROYAL DINNER!
IT'S KINDA BIG FOR YOU, HEDDA... BUT IF I PIN IT HERE AND THERE, IT JUST MIGHT WORK.
HEDDA--CAN'T YOU HOLD STILL FOR A SECOND?
BUT I LIKE MY FRECKLES-- HRNN... HRNN...
ATCHOO!
ACK!
OW LONG HAS IT BEEN SINCE YOU BRUSHED YOUR HAIR, HEDDA? I CAN'T GET A COMB THROUGH IT.
OH, UH... HMM...
MR. HANSEN... SHE CAN BORROW ONE OF MY BOWS IF SHE WANTS.
R-REALLY? BUT YOU DON'T LET ANYONE TOUCH YOUR BOWS!
BUT I WANT IT BACK--AND WASHED--WHEN YOU'RE DONE WITH IT.

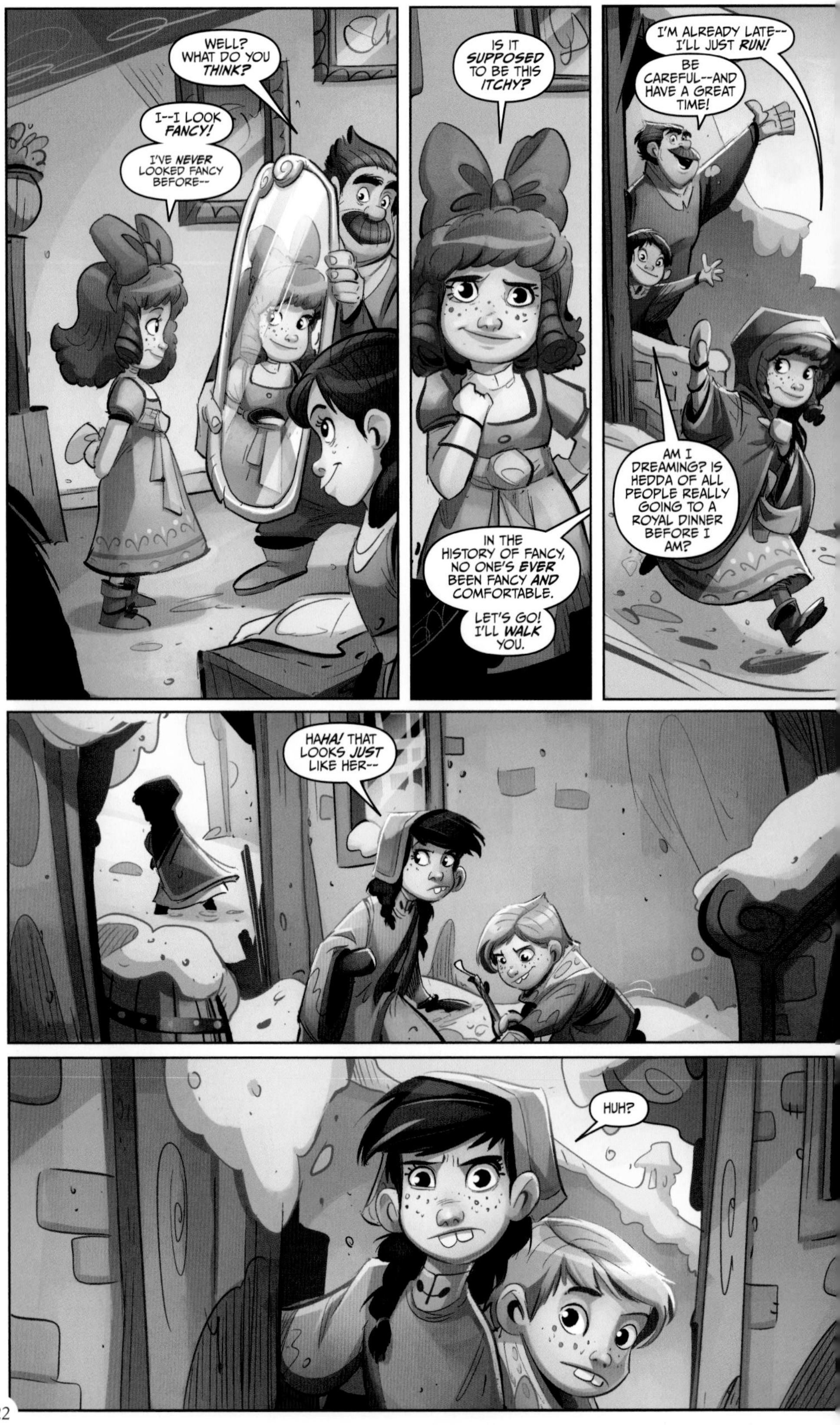
WELL? WHAT DO YOU *THINK?*
I--I LOOK *FANCY!*
I'VE *NEVER* LOOKED FANCY BEFORE--
IS IT *SUPPOSED* TO BE THIS *ITCHY?*
IN THE HISTORY OF FANCY, NO ONE'S *EVER* BEEN FANCY *AND* COMFORTABLE.
LET'S GO! I'LL *WALK* YOU.
I'M ALREADY LATE-- I'LL JUST *RUN!*
BE CAREFUL--AND HAVE A GREAT TIME!
AM I DREAMING? IS HEDDA OF ALL PEOPLE REALLY GOING TO A ROYAL DINNER BEFORE I AM?
HA*HA!* THAT LOOKS *JUST* LIKE HER--
HUH?

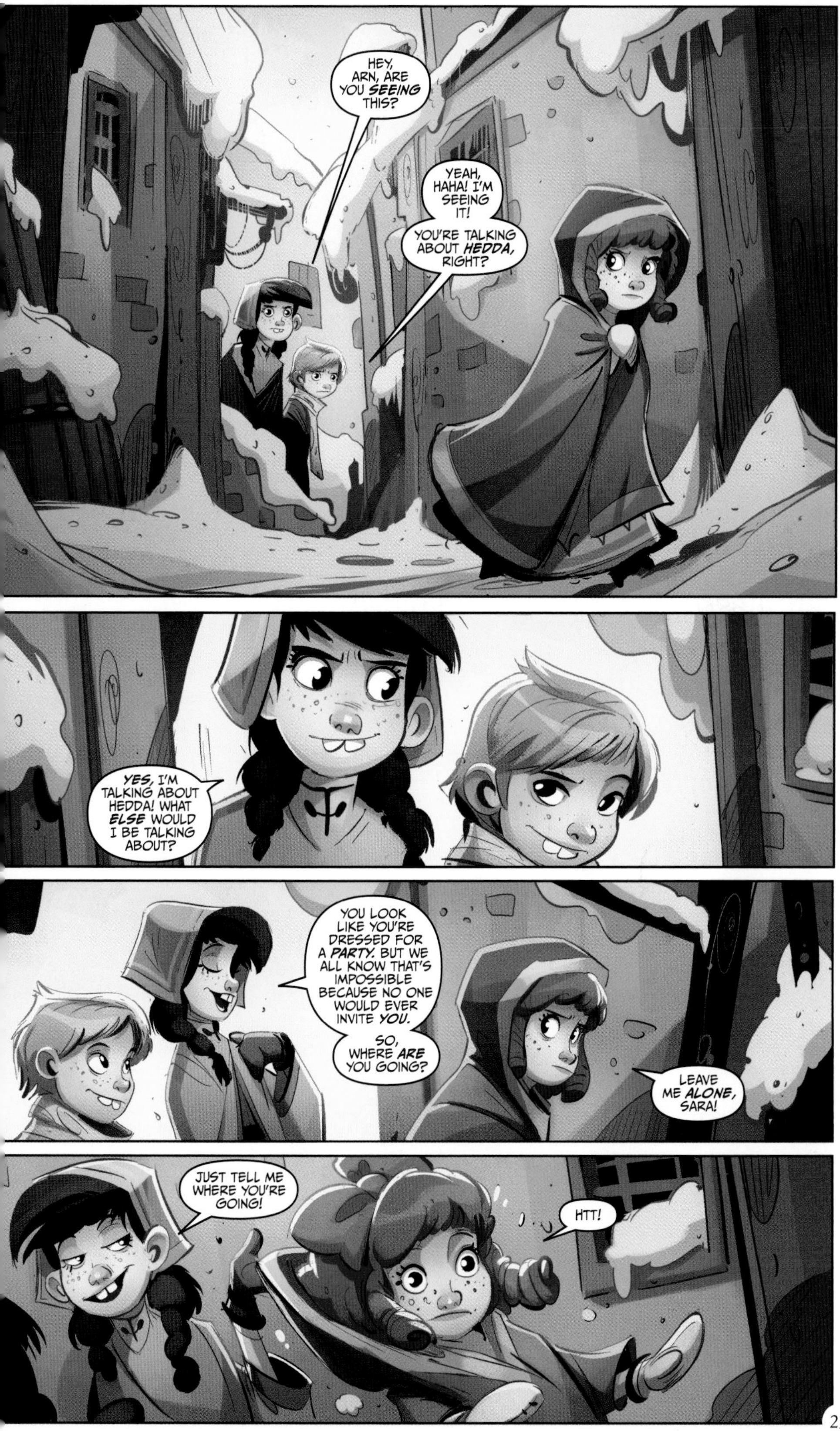
HEY, ARN, ARE YOU SEEING THIS?
YEAH, HAHA! I'M SEEING IT!
YOU'RE TALKING ABOUT HEDDA, RIGHT?
YES, I'M TALKING ABOUT HEDDA! WHAT ELSE WOULD I BE TALKING ABOUT?
YOU LOOK LIKE YOU'RE DRESSED FOR A PARTY. BUT WE ALL KNOW THAT'S IMPOSSIBLE BECAUSE NO ONE WOULD EVER INVITE YOU.
SO, WHERE ARE YOU GOING?
LEAVE ME ALONE, SARA!
JUST TELL ME WHERE YOU'RE GOING!
HTT!

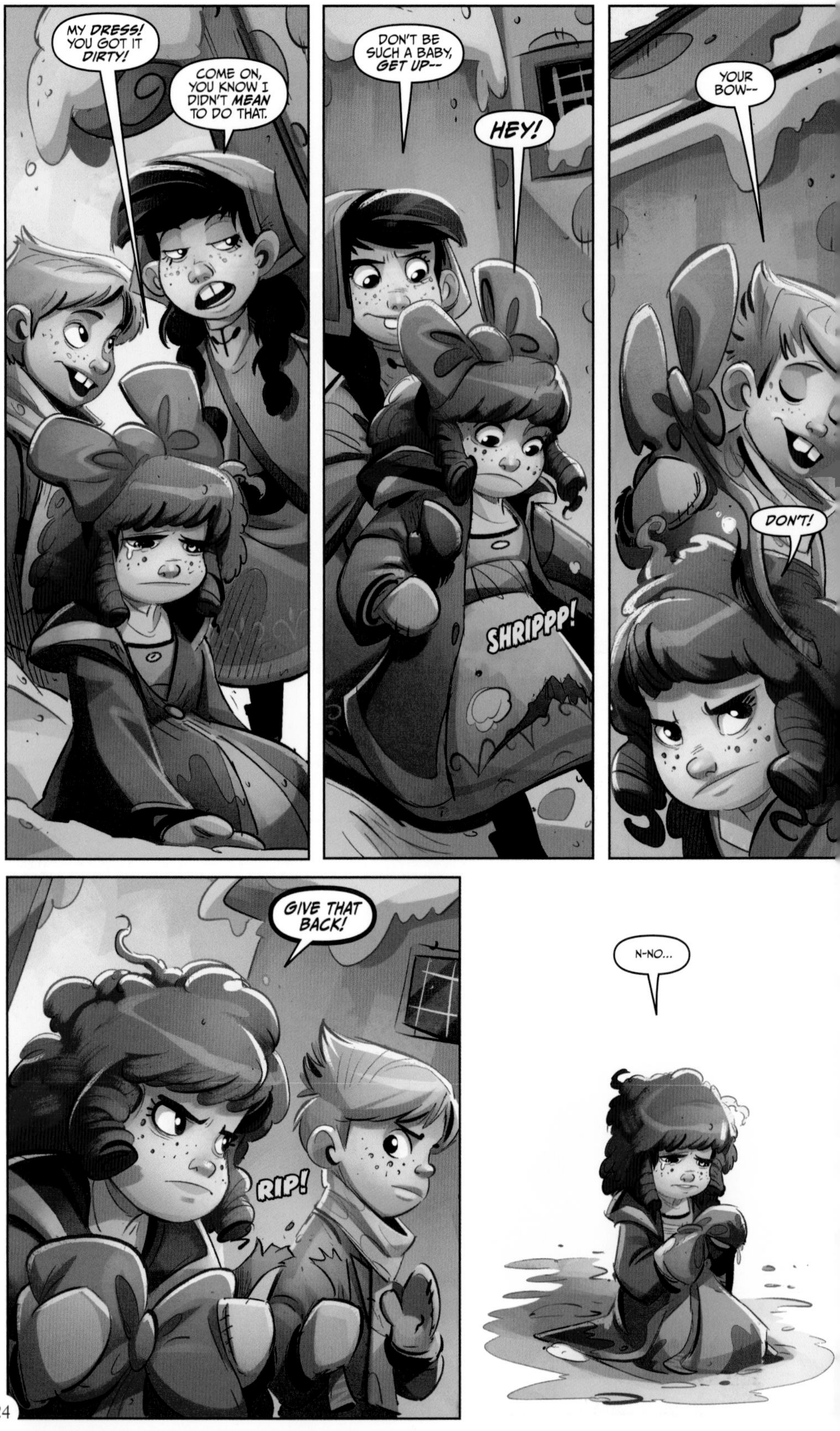
MY DRESS! YOU GOT IT DIRTY!
COME ON, YOU KNOW I DIDN'T MEAN TO DO THAT.
DON'T BE SUCH A BABY, GET UP--
HEY!
SHRIPPP!
YOUR BOW--
DON'T!
GIVE THAT BACK!
RIP!
N-NO...

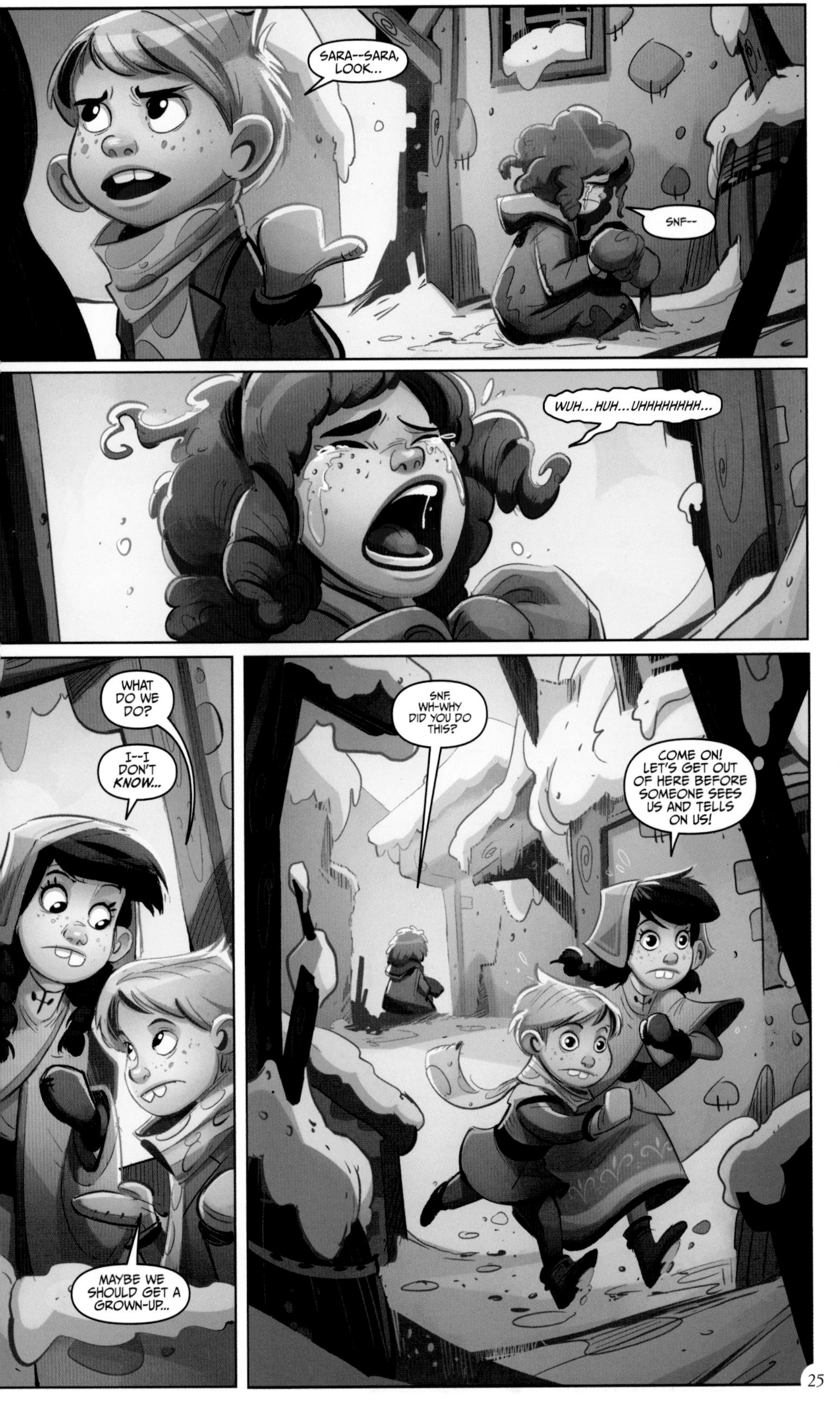
SARA--SARA, LOOK...
SNF--
WUH...HUH...UHHHHHHHH...
WHAT DO WE DO?
I--I DON'T KNOW...
MAYBE WE SHOULD GET A GROWN-UP...
SNF. WH-WHY DID YOU DO THIS?
COME ON! LET'S GET OUT OF HERE BEFORE SOMEONE SEES US AND TELLS ON US!

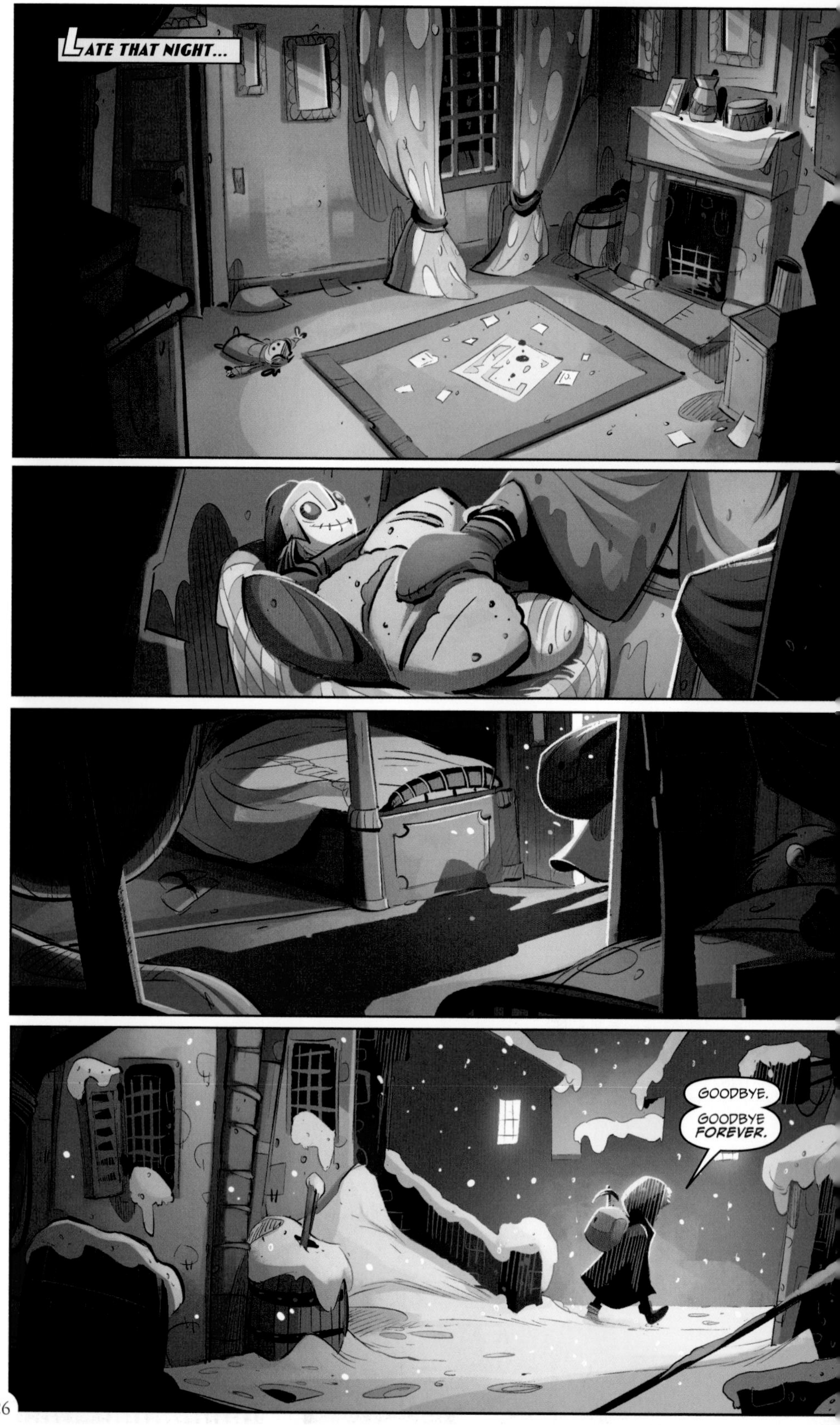
LATE THAT NIGHT...
GOODBYE. GOODBYE FOREVER.

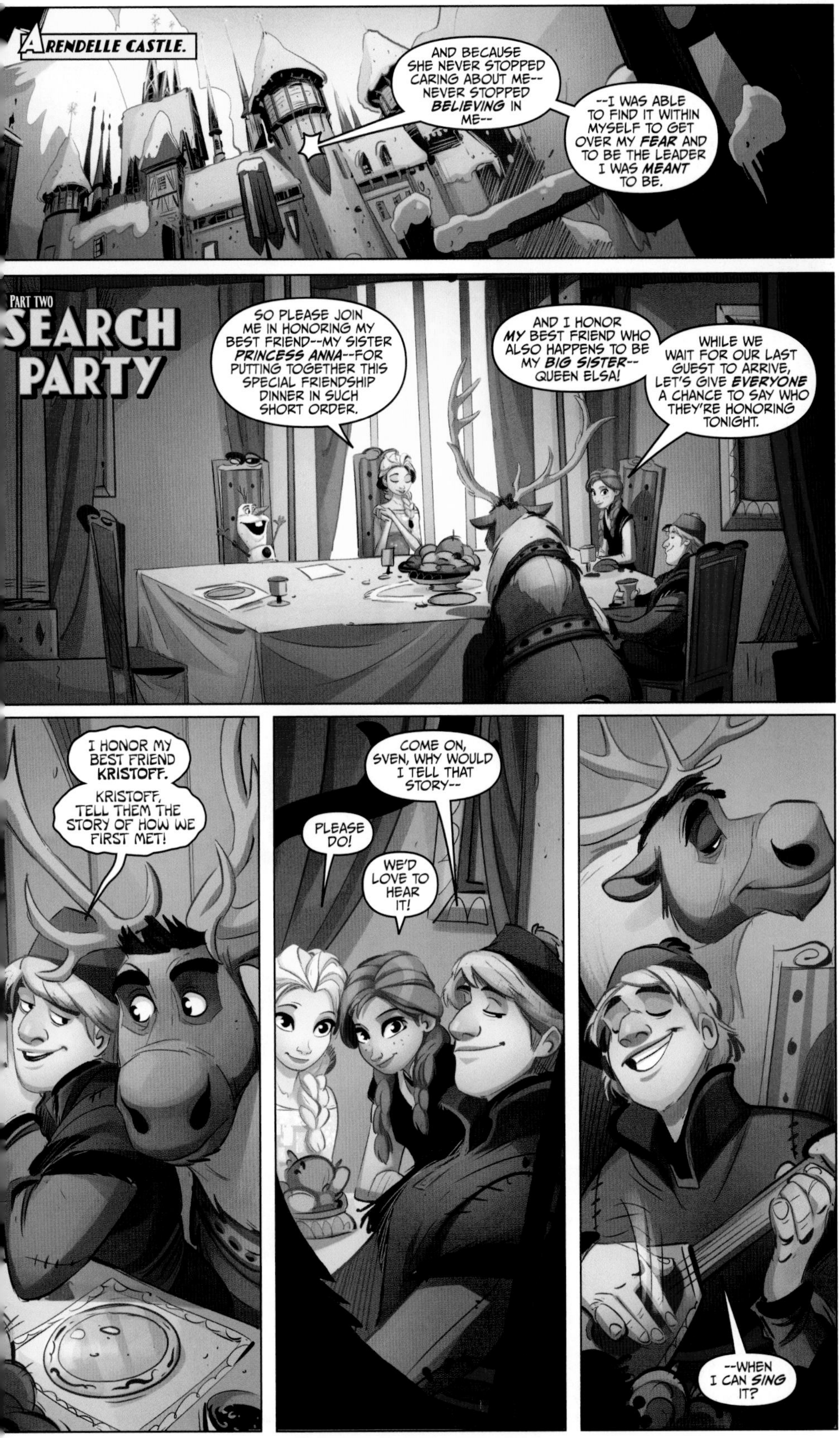
ARENDELLE CASTLE.
AND BECAUSE SHE NEVER STOPPED CARING ABOUT ME-- NEVER STOPPED BELIEVING IN ME--
--I WAS ABLE TO FIND IT WITHIN MYSELF TO GET OVER MY FEAR AND TO BE THE LEADER I WAS MEANT TO BE.
PART TWO
SEARCH PARTY
SO PLEASE JOIN ME IN HONORING MY BEST FRIEND--MY SISTER PRINCESS ANNA--FOR PUTTING TOGETHER THIS SPECIAL FRIENDSHIP DINNER IN SUCH SHORT ORDER.
AND I HONOR MY BEST FRIEND WHO ALSO HAPPENS TO BE MY BIG SISTER-- QUEEN ELSA!
WHILE WE WAIT FOR OUR LAST GUEST TO ARRIVE, LET'S GIVE EVERYONE A CHANCE TO SAY WHO THEY'RE HONORING TONIGHT.
I HONOR MY BEST FRIEND KRISTOFF.
KRISTOFF, TELL THEM THE STORY OF HOW WE FIRST MET!
COME ON, SVEN, WHY WOULD I TELL THAT STORY--
PLEASE DO!
WE'D LOVE TO HEAR IT!
--WHEN I CAN SING IT?

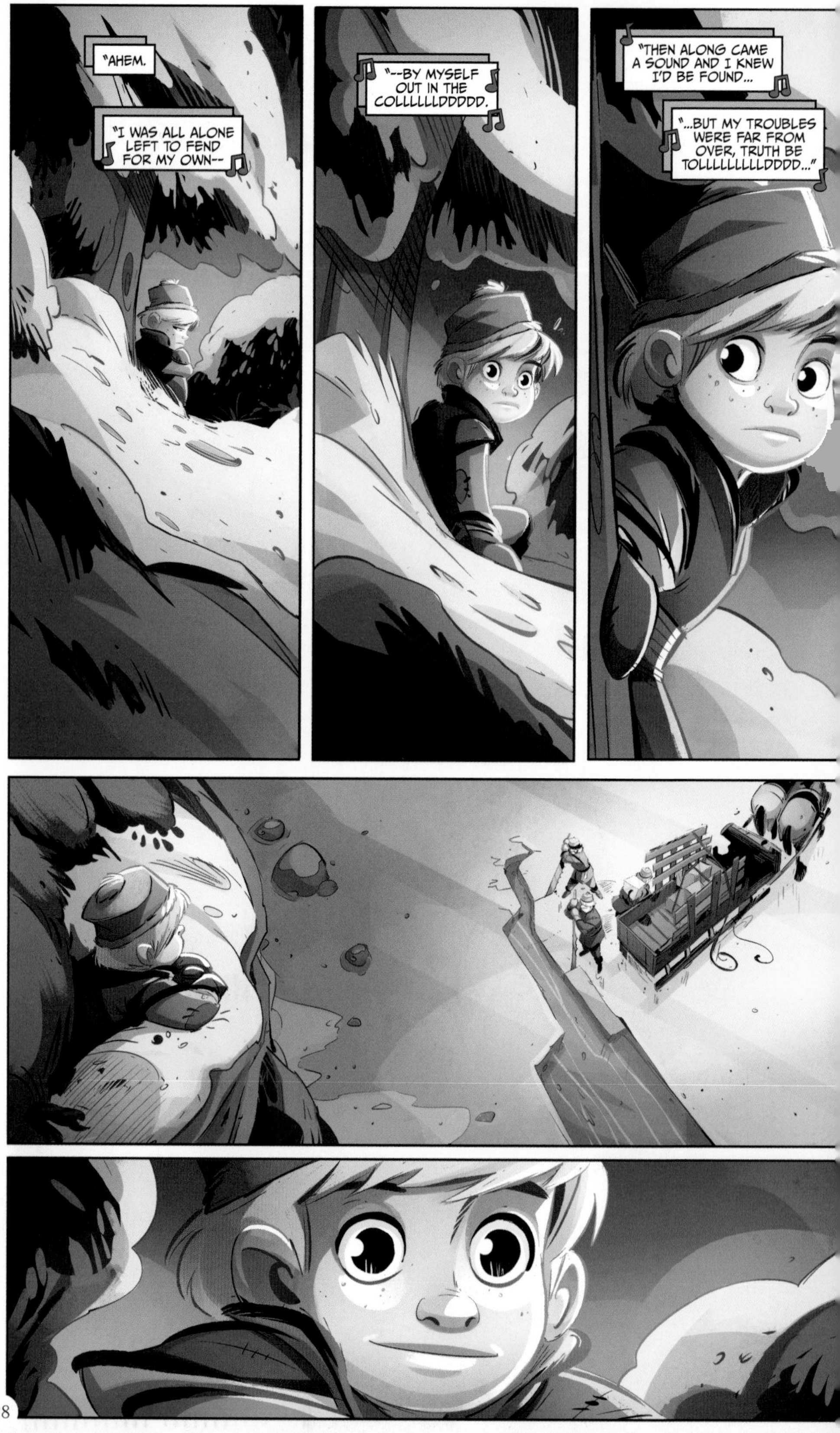
"AHEM.
"I WAS ALL ALONE LEFT TO FEND FOR MY OWN--
"--BY MYSELF OUT IN THE COLLLLLLLDDDDD.
"THEN ALONG CAME A SOUND AND I KNEW I'D BE FOUND...
"...BUT MY TROUBLES WERE FAR FROM OVER, TRUTH BE TOLLLLLLLLLLDDDD..."

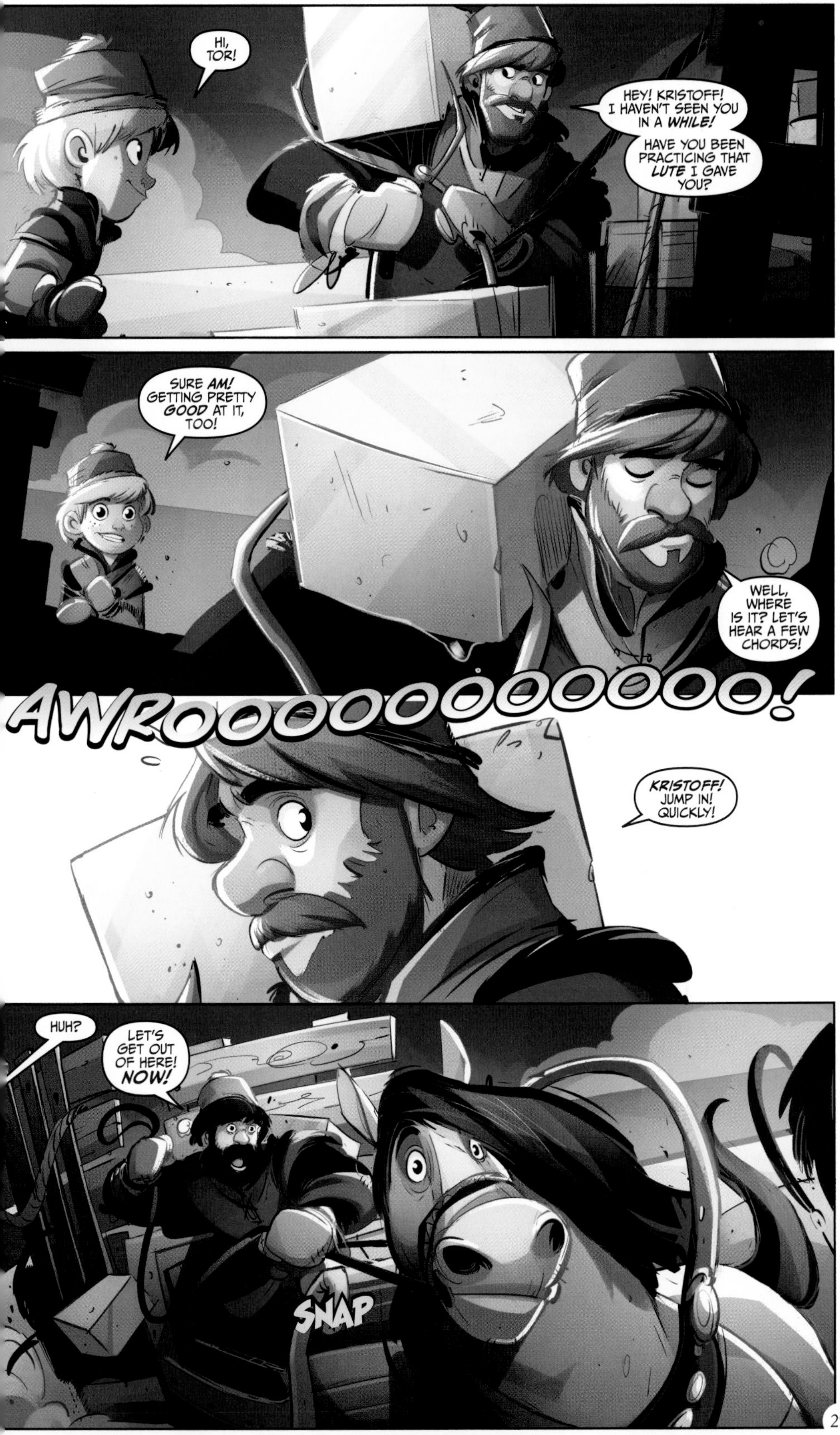
HI, TOR!
HEY! KRISTOFF! I HAVEN'T SEEN YOU IN A *WHILE!*
HAVE YOU BEEN PRACTICING THAT *LUTE* I GAVE YOU?
SURE *AM!* GETTING PRETTY *GOOD* AT IT, TOO!
WELL, WHERE IS IT? LET'S HEAR A FEW CHORDS!
AWROOOOOOOOOOOO!
KRISTOFF! JUMP IN! QUICKLY!
HUH?
LET'S GET OUT OF HERE! *NOW!*
SNAP

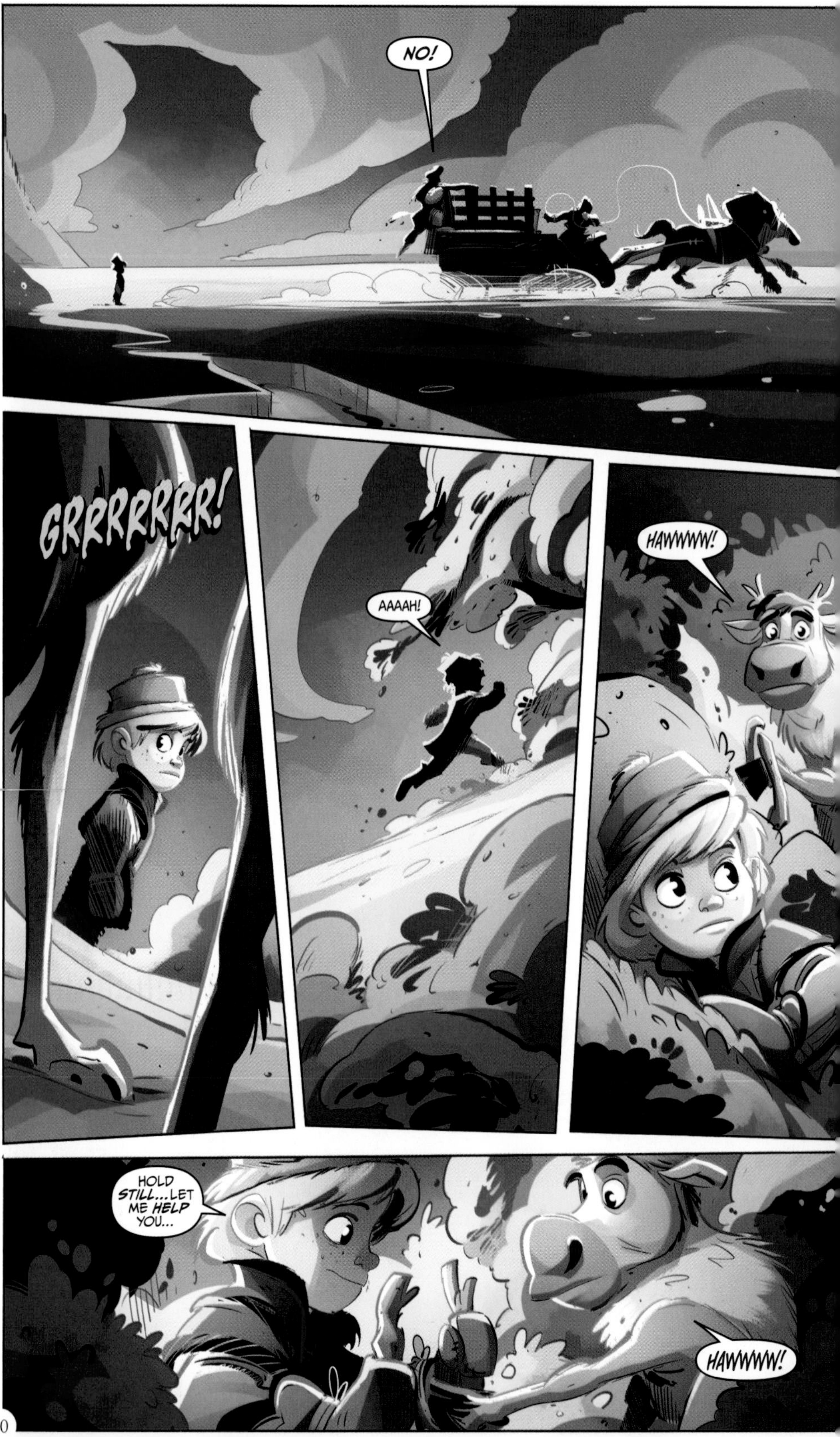
NO!
GRRRRRRR!
AAAAH!
HAWWWW!
HOLD STILL...LET ME HELP YOU...
HAWWWW!

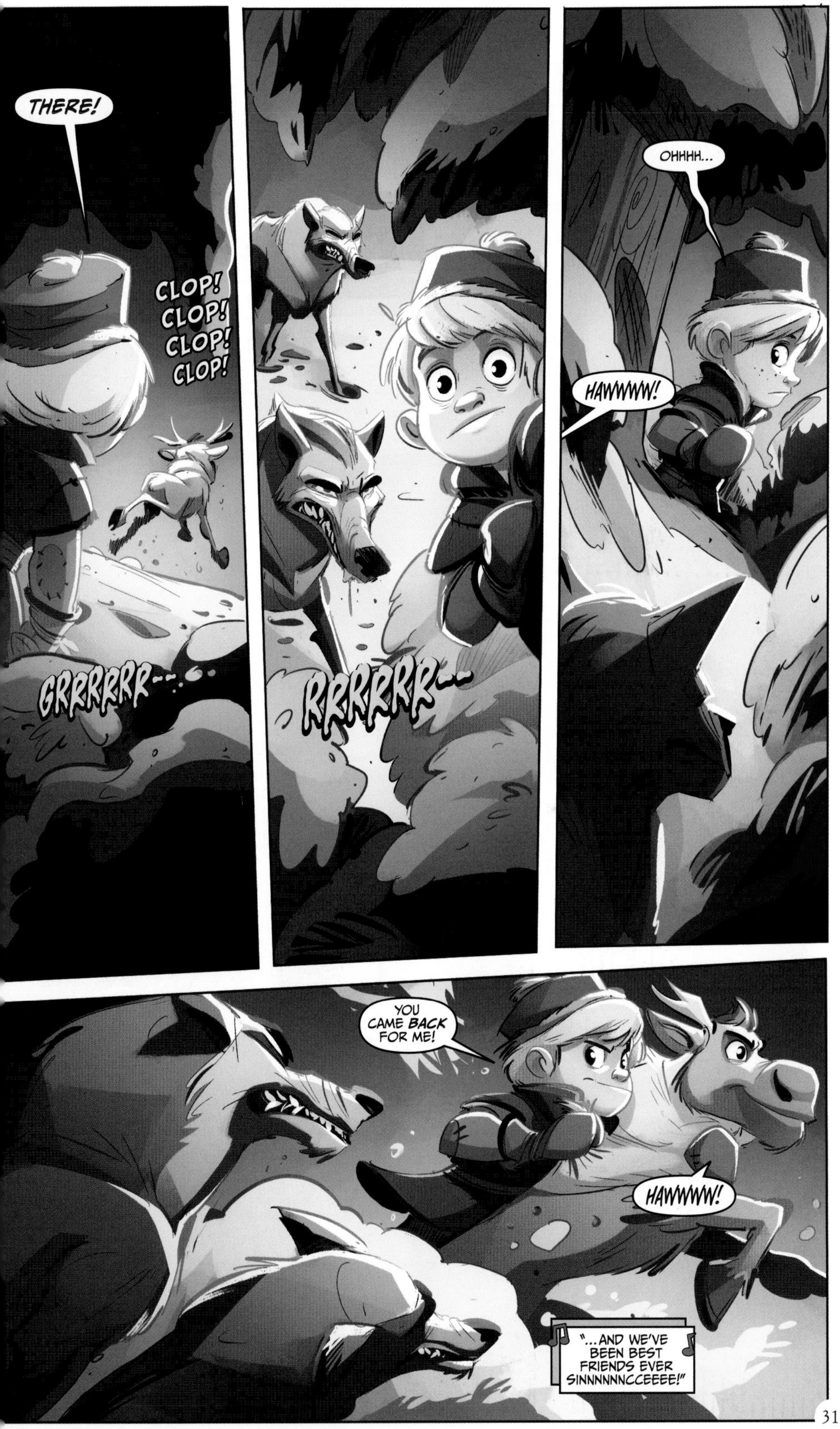
THERE!
CLOP! CLOP! CLOP! CLOP!
GRRRRRR--
RRRRRR--
OHHHH...
HAWWWW!
YOU CAME BACK FOR ME!
HAWWWW!
"...AND WE'VE BEEN BEST FRIENDS EVER SINNNNNNCCEEEE!"

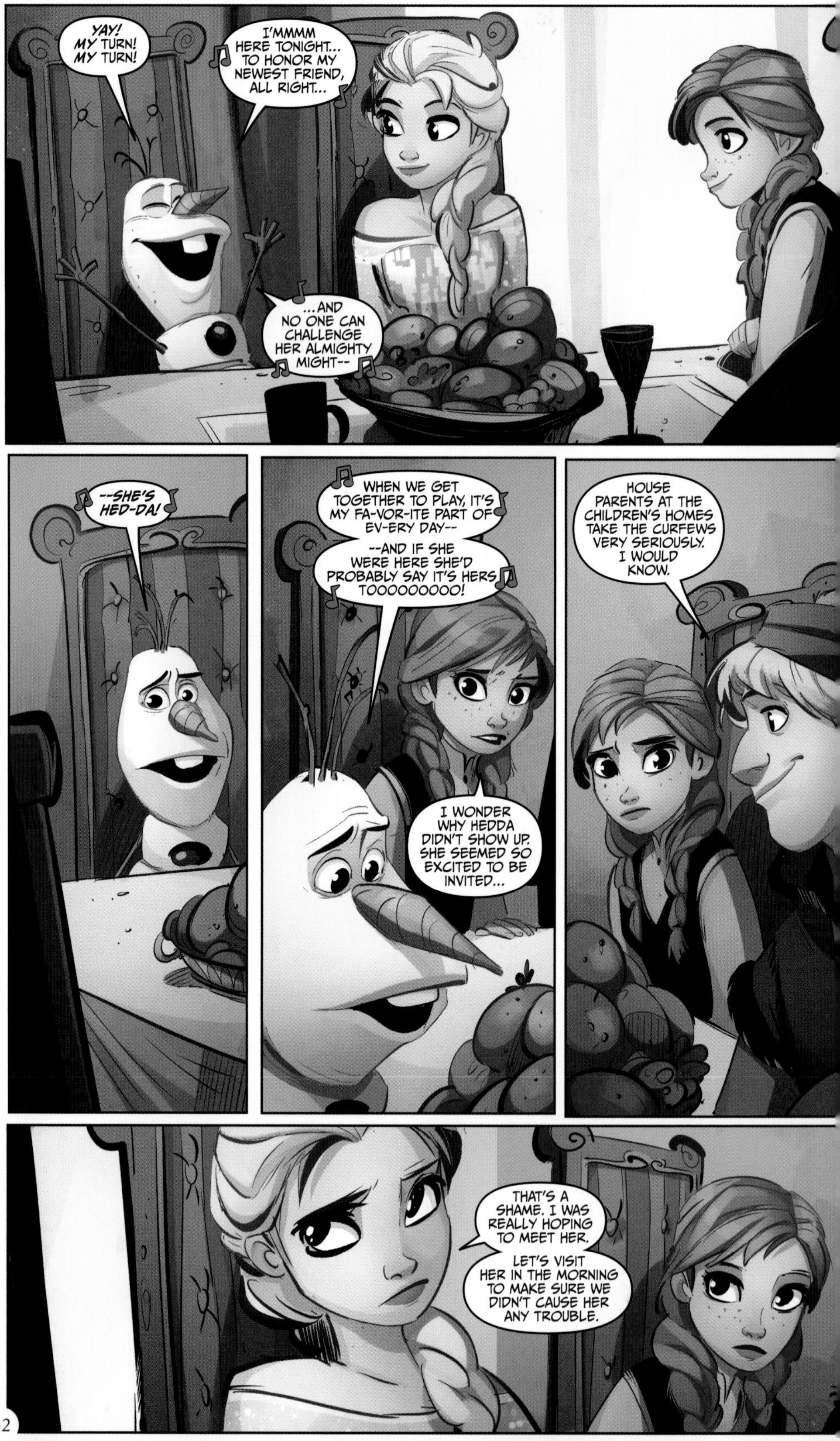
YAY! MY TURN! MY TURN!
I'MMMM HERE TONIGHT... TO HONOR MY NEWEST FRIEND, ALL RIGHT...
...AND NO ONE CAN CHALLENGE HER ALMIGHTY MIGHT--
--SHE'S HED-DA!
WHEN WE GET TOGETHER TO PLAY, IT'S MY FA-VOR-ITE PART OF EV-ERY DAY--
--AND IF SHE WERE HERE SHE'D PROBABLY SAY IT'S HERS TOOOOOOOOO!
I WONDER WHY HEDDA DIDN'T SHOW UP. SHE SEEMED SO EXCITED TO BE INVITED...
HOUSE PARENTS AT THE CHILDREN'S HOMES TAKE THE CURFEWS VERY SERIOUSLY. I WOULD KNOW.
THAT'S A SHAME. I WAS REALLY HOPING TO MEET HER.
LET'S VISIT HER IN THE MORNING TO MAKE SURE WE DIDN'T CAUSE HER ANY TROUBLE.

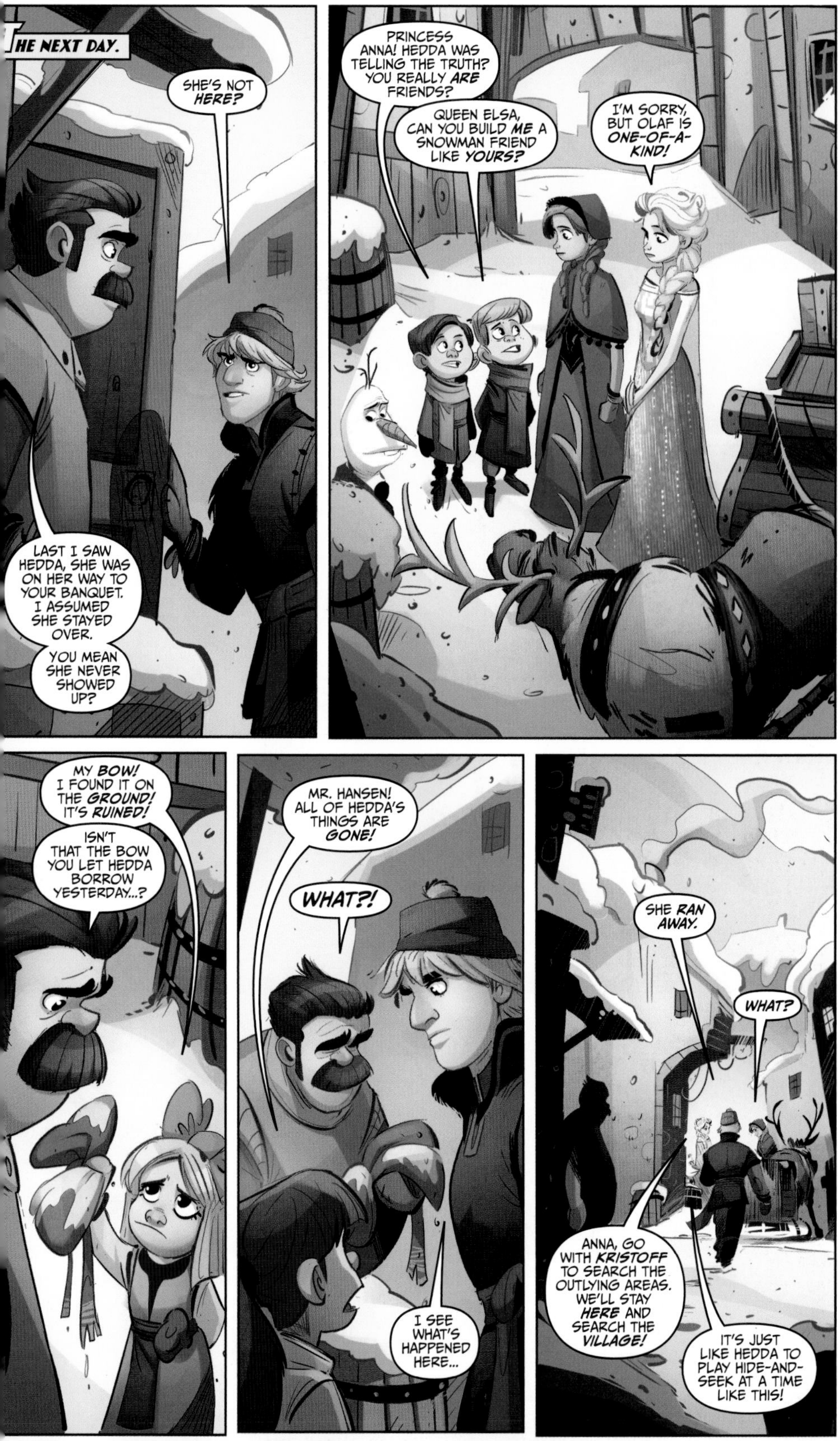
THE NEXT DAY.
SHE'S NOT HERE?
LAST I SAW HEDDA, SHE WAS ON HER WAY TO YOUR BANQUET. I ASSUMED SHE STAYED OVER.
YOU MEAN SHE NEVER SHOWED UP?
PRINCESS ANNA! HEDDA WAS TELLING THE TRUTH? YOU REALLY ARE FRIENDS?
QUEEN ELSA, CAN YOU BUILD ME A SNOWMAN FRIEND LIKE YOURS?
I'M SORRY, BUT OLAF IS ONE-OF-A-KIND!
MY BOW! I FOUND IT ON THE GROUND! IT'S RUINED!
ISN'T THAT THE BOW YOU LET HEDDA BORROW YESTERDAY...?
MR. HANSEN! ALL OF HEDDA'S THINGS ARE GONE!
WHAT?!
I SEE WHAT'S HAPPENED HERE...
SHE RAN AWAY.
WHAT?
ANNA, GO WITH KRISTOFF TO SEARCH THE OUTLYING AREAS. WE'LL STAY HERE AND SEARCH THE VILLAGE!
IT'S JUST LIKE HEDDA TO PLAY HIDE-AND-SEEK AT A TIME LIKE THIS!

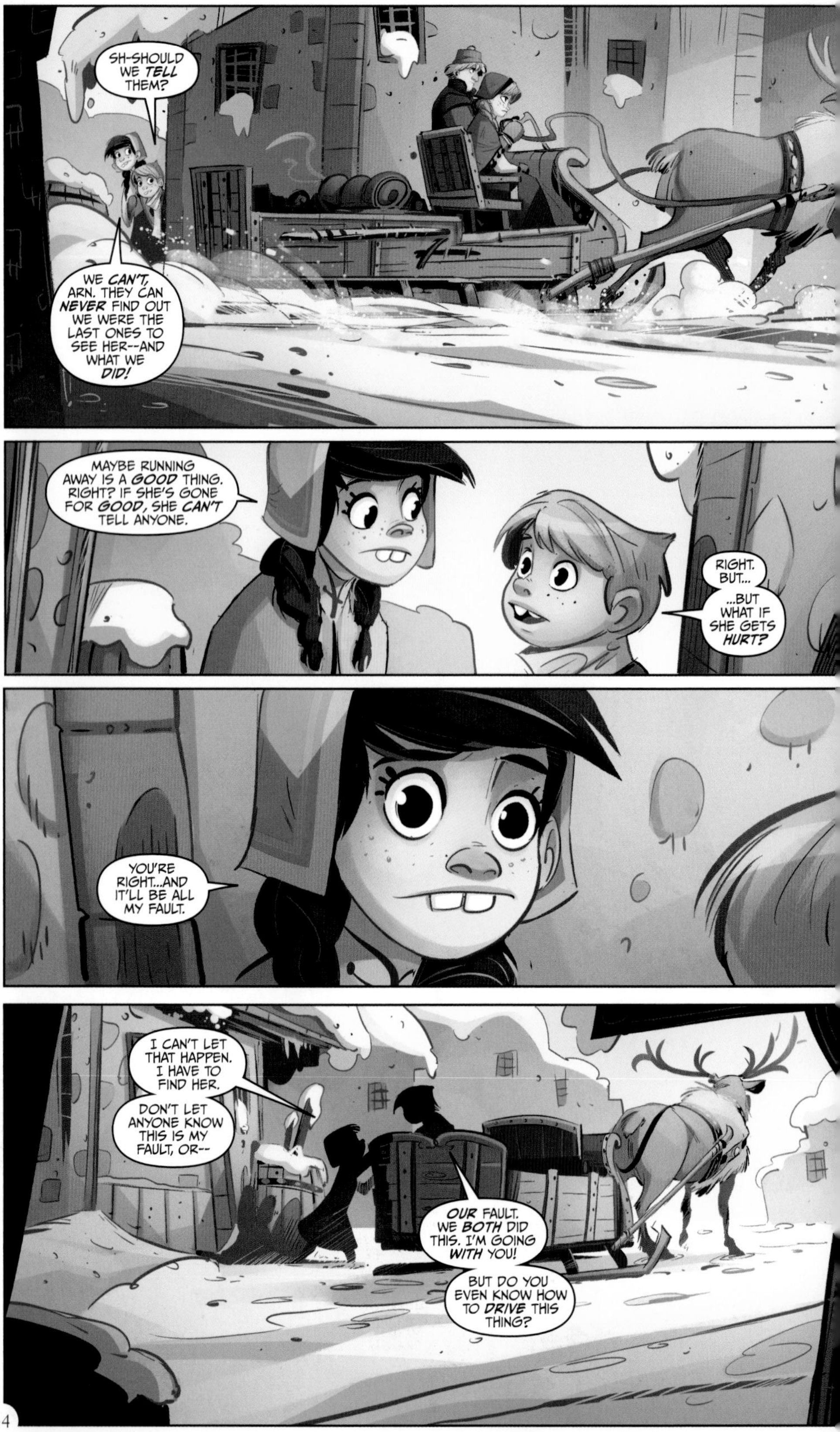
SH-SHOULD WE TELL THEM?
WE CAN'T, ARN. THEY CAN NEVER FIND OUT WE WERE THE LAST ONES TO SEE HER--AND WHAT WE DID!
MAYBE RUNNING AWAY IS A GOOD THING. RIGHT? IF SHE'S GONE FOR GOOD, SHE CAN'T TELL ANYONE.
RIGHT. BUT...
...BUT WHAT IF SHE GETS HURT?
YOU'RE RIGHT...AND IT'LL BE ALL MY FAULT.
I CAN'T LET THAT HAPPEN. I HAVE TO FIND HER.
DON'T LET ANYONE KNOW THIS IS MY FAULT, OR--
OUR FAULT. WE BOTH DID THIS. I'M GOING WITH YOU!
BUT DO YOU EVEN KNOW HOW TO DRIVE THIS THING?

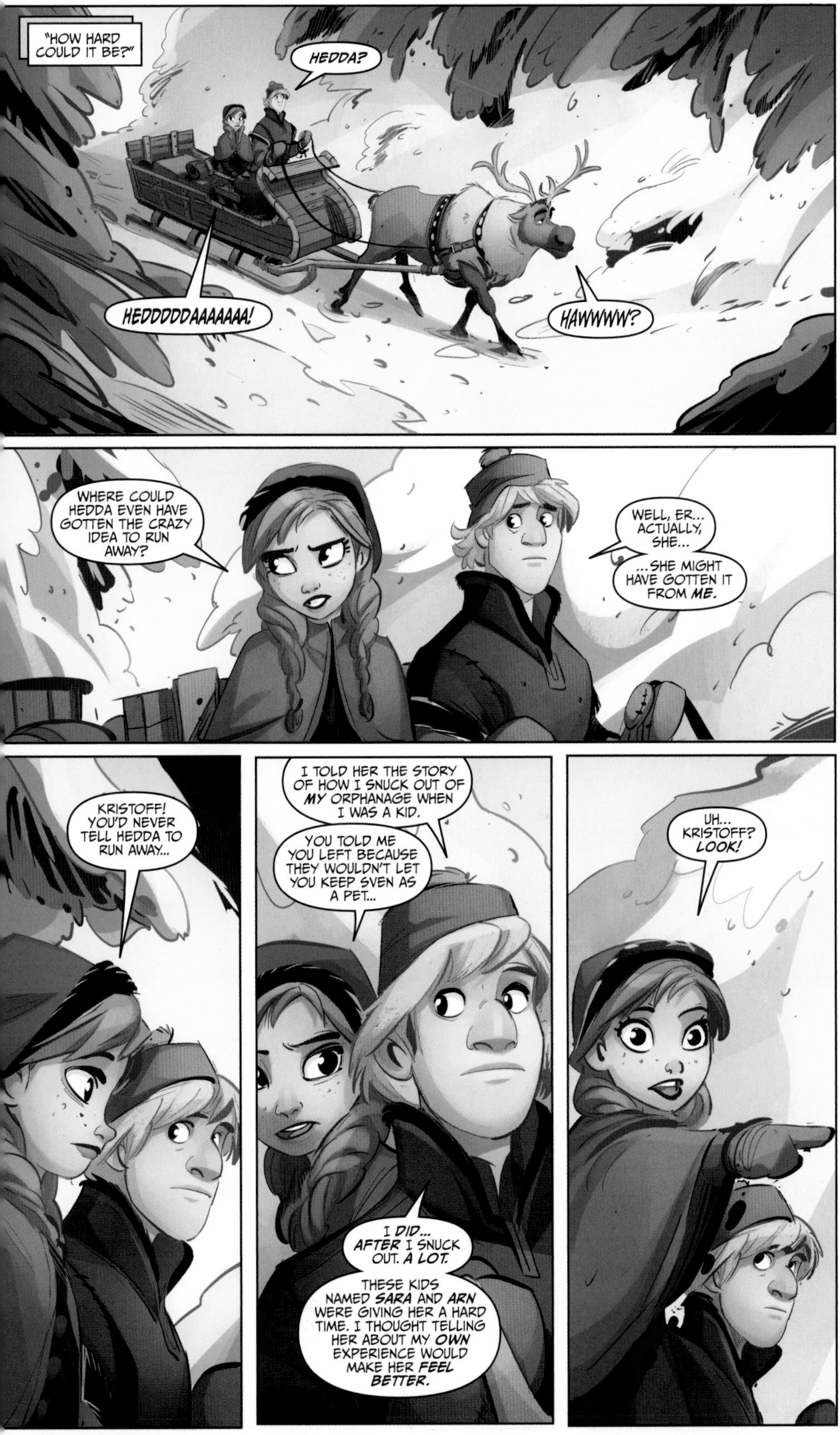
"HOW HARD COULD IT BE?"
HEDDA?
HEDDDDDAAAAAAA!
HAWWWW?
WHERE COULD HEDDA EVEN HAVE GOTTEN THE CRAZY IDEA TO RUN AWAY?
WELL, ER... ACTUALLY, SHE...
...SHE MIGHT HAVE GOTTEN IT FROM ME.
KRISTOFF! YOU'D NEVER TELL HEDDA TO RUN AWAY...
I TOLD HER THE STORY OF HOW I SNUCK OUT OF MY ORPHANAGE WHEN I WAS A KID.
YOU TOLD ME YOU LEFT BECAUSE THEY WOULDN'T LET YOU KEEP SVEN AS A PET...
I DID... AFTER I SNUCK OUT. A LOT.
THESE KIDS NAMED SARA AND ARN WERE GIVING HER A HARD TIME. I THOUGHT TELLING HER ABOUT MY OWN EXPERIENCE WOULD MAKE HER FEEL BETTER.
UH... KRISTOFF? LOOK!

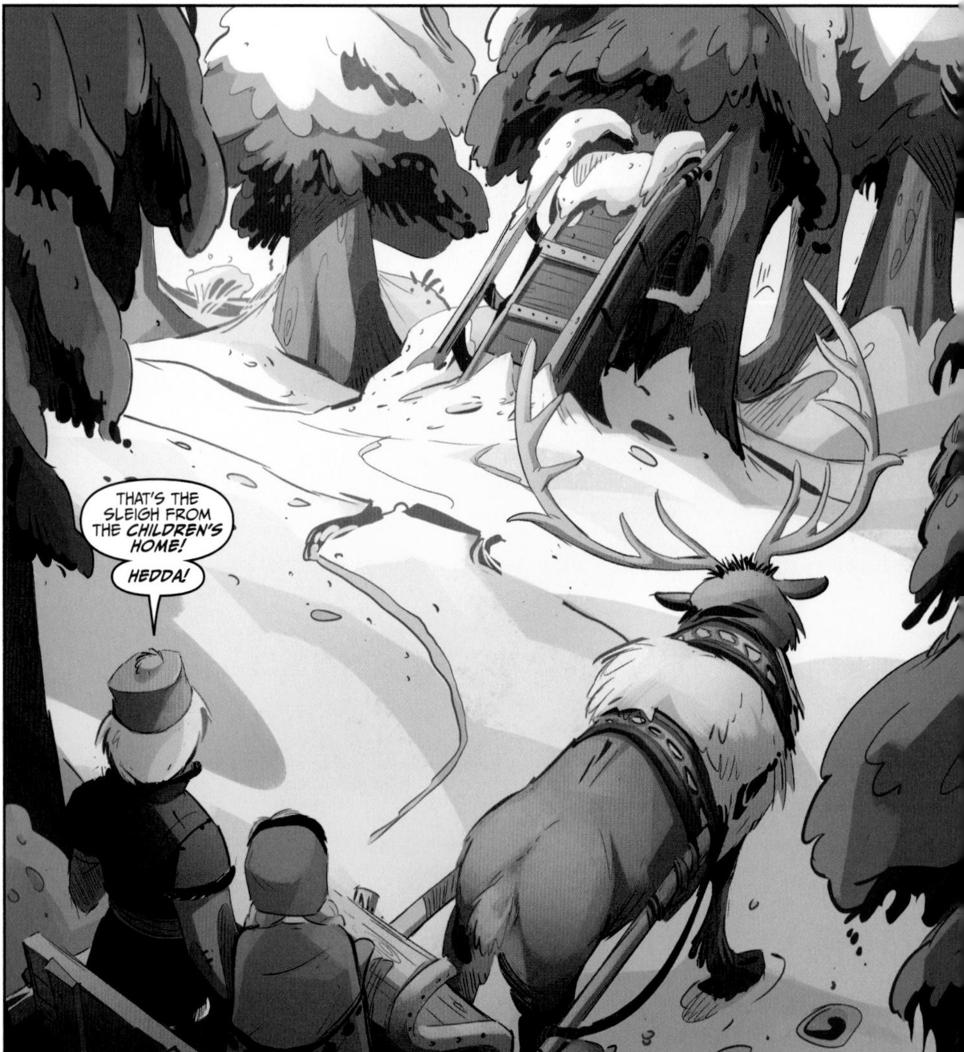
THAT'S THE SLEIGH FROM THE *CHILDREN'S HOME!*
HEDDA!

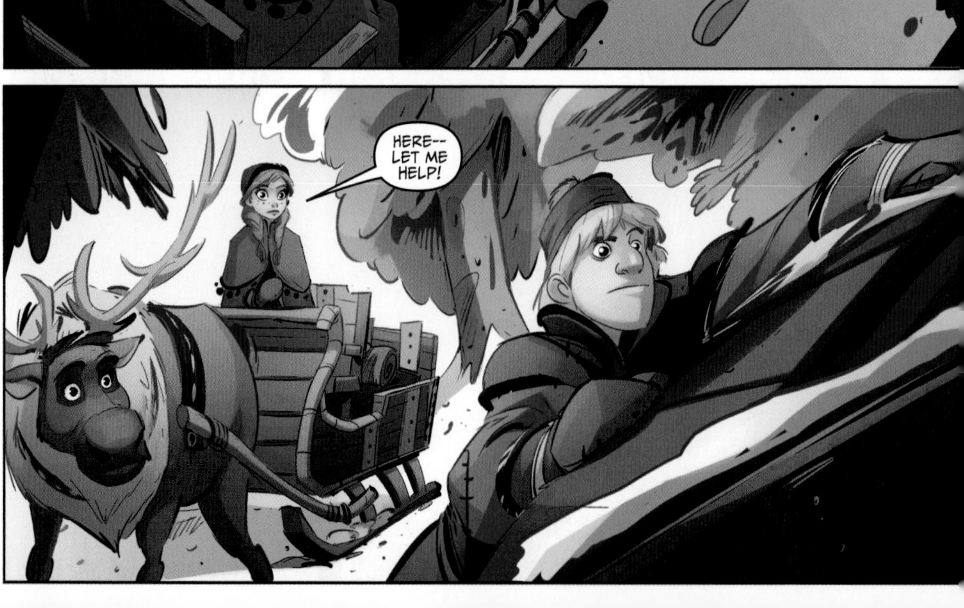
HERE-- LET ME HELP!

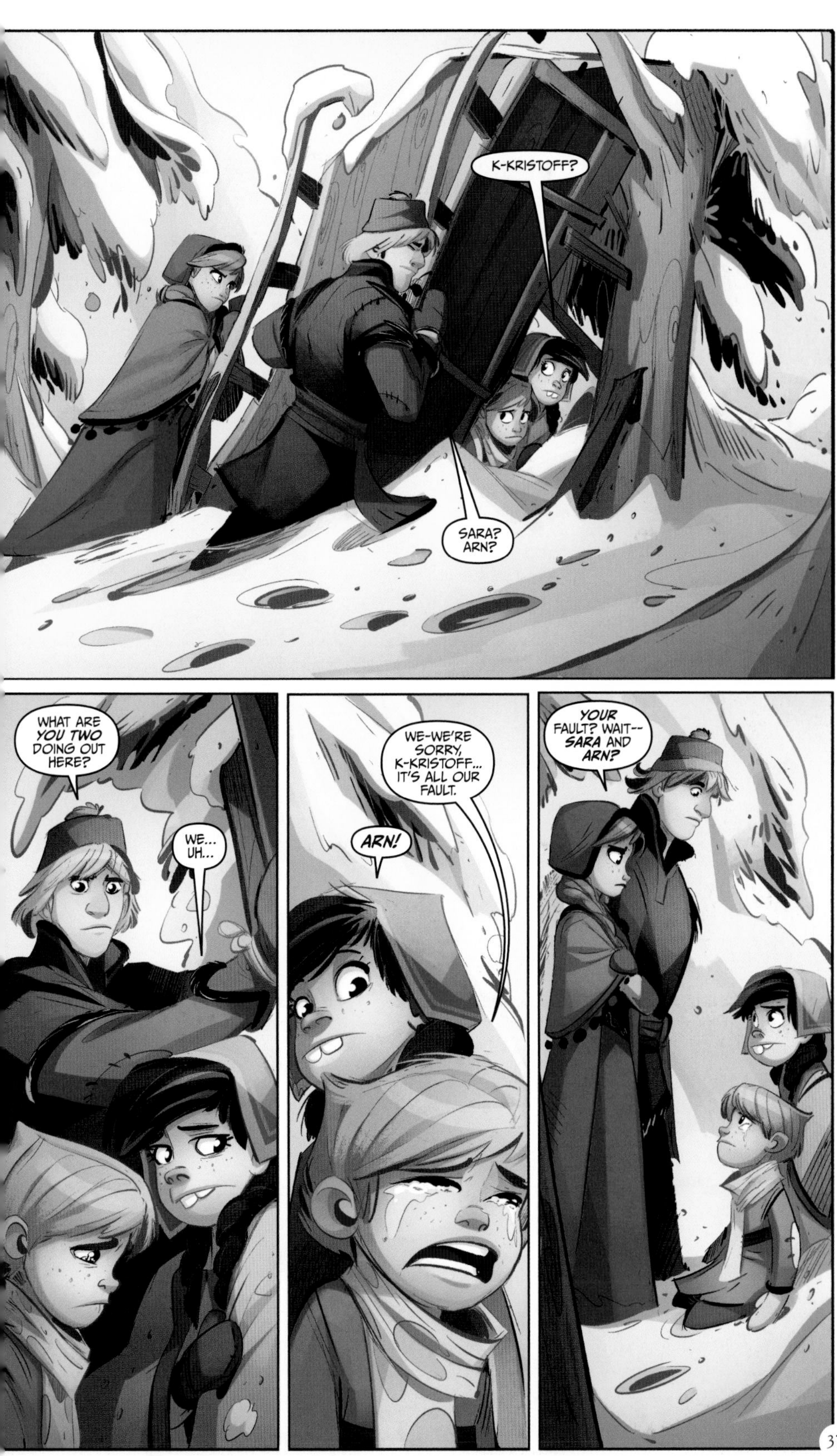
K-KRISTOFF?
SARA? ARN?
WHAT ARE *YOU TWO* DOING OUT HERE?
WE... UH...
WE-WE'RE SORRY, K-KRISTOFF... IT'S ALL OUR FAULT.
ARN!
YOUR FAULT? WAIT-- *SARA* AND *ARN?*

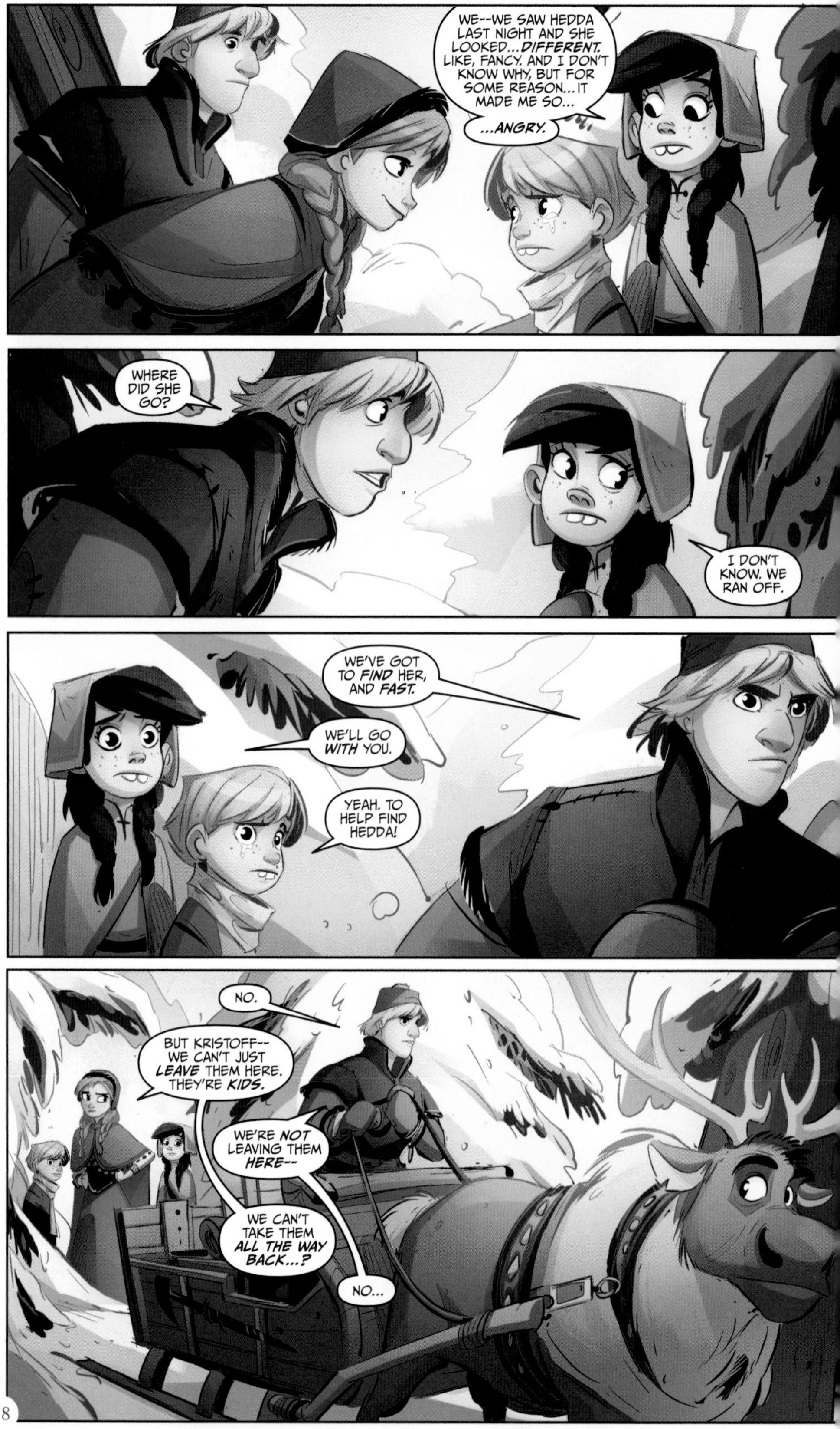
WE--WE SAW HEDDA LAST NIGHT AND SHE LOOKED...*DIFFERENT.* LIKE, FANCY. AND I DON'T KNOW WHY, BUT FOR SOME REASON...IT MADE ME SO...
...*ANGRY.*
WHERE DID SHE GO?
I DON'T KNOW. WE RAN OFF.
WE'VE GOT TO *FIND* HER, AND *FAST.*
WE'LL GO *WITH* YOU.
YEAH. TO HELP FIND HEDDA!
NO.
BUT KRISTOFF-- WE CAN'T JUST *LEAVE* THEM HERE. THEY'RE *KIDS.*
WE'RE *NOT* LEAVING THEM *HERE--*
WE CAN'T TAKE THEM *ALL THE WAY BACK...?*
NO...

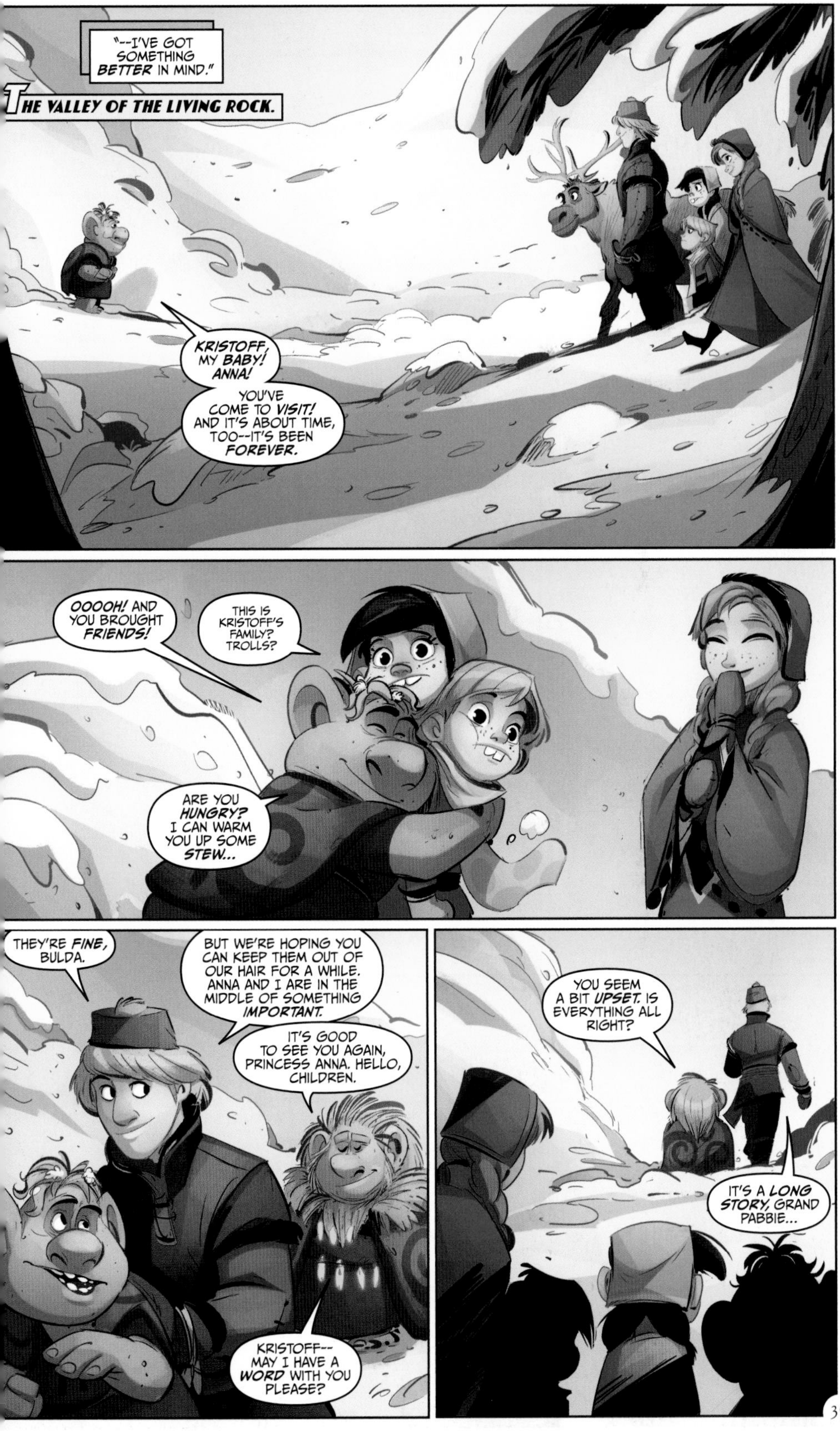
"--I'VE GOT SOMETHING BETTER IN MIND."
THE VALLEY OF THE LIVING ROCK.
KRISTOFF, MY BABY! ANNA!
YOU'VE COME TO VISIT! AND IT'S ABOUT TIME, TOO--IT'S BEEN FOREVER.
OOOOH! AND YOU BROUGHT FRIENDS!
THIS IS KRISTOFF'S FAMILY? TROLLS?
ARE YOU HUNGRY? I CAN WARM YOU UP SOME STEW...
THEY'RE FINE, BULDA.
BUT WE'RE HOPING YOU CAN KEEP THEM OUT OF OUR HAIR FOR A WHILE. ANNA AND I ARE IN THE MIDDLE OF SOMETHING IMPORTANT.
IT'S GOOD TO SEE YOU AGAIN, PRINCESS ANNA. HELLO, CHILDREN.
KRISTOFF-- MAY I HAVE A WORD WITH YOU PLEASE?
YOU SEEM A BIT UPSET. IS EVERYTHING ALL RIGHT?
IT'S A LONG STORY, GRAND PABBIE...

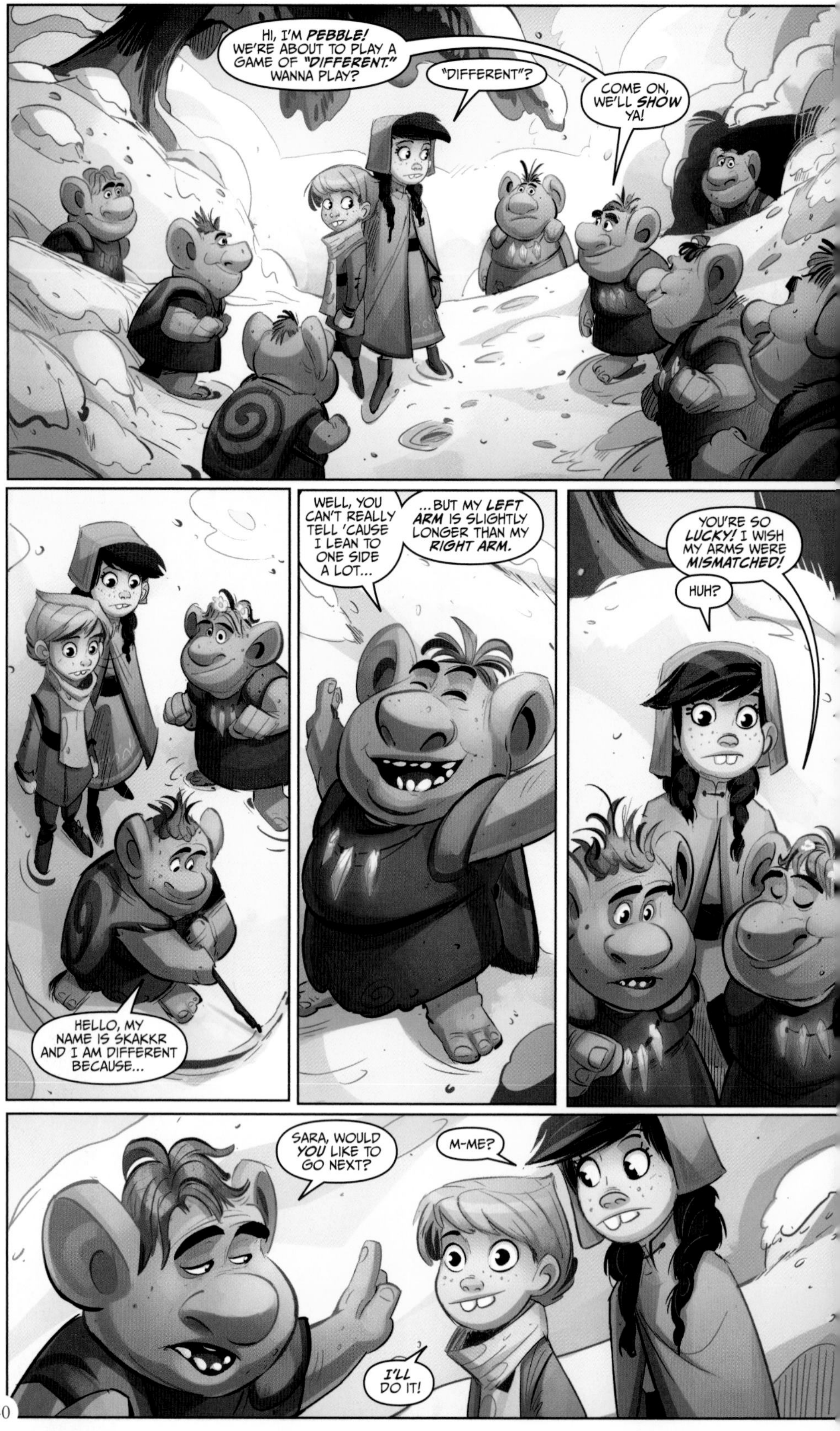
HI, I'M PEBBLE! WE'RE ABOUT TO PLAY A GAME OF "DIFFERENT." WANNA PLAY?
"DIFFERENT"?
COME ON, WE'LL SHOW YA!
HELLO, MY NAME IS SKAKKR AND I AM DIFFERENT BECAUSE...
WELL, YOU CAN'T REALLY TELL 'CAUSE I LEAN TO ONE SIDE A LOT...
...BUT MY LEFT ARM IS SLIGHTLY LONGER THAN MY RIGHT ARM.
YOU'RE SO LUCKY! I WISH MY ARMS WERE MISMATCHED!
HUH?
SARA, WOULD YOU LIKE TO GO NEXT?
M-ME?
I'LL DO IT!

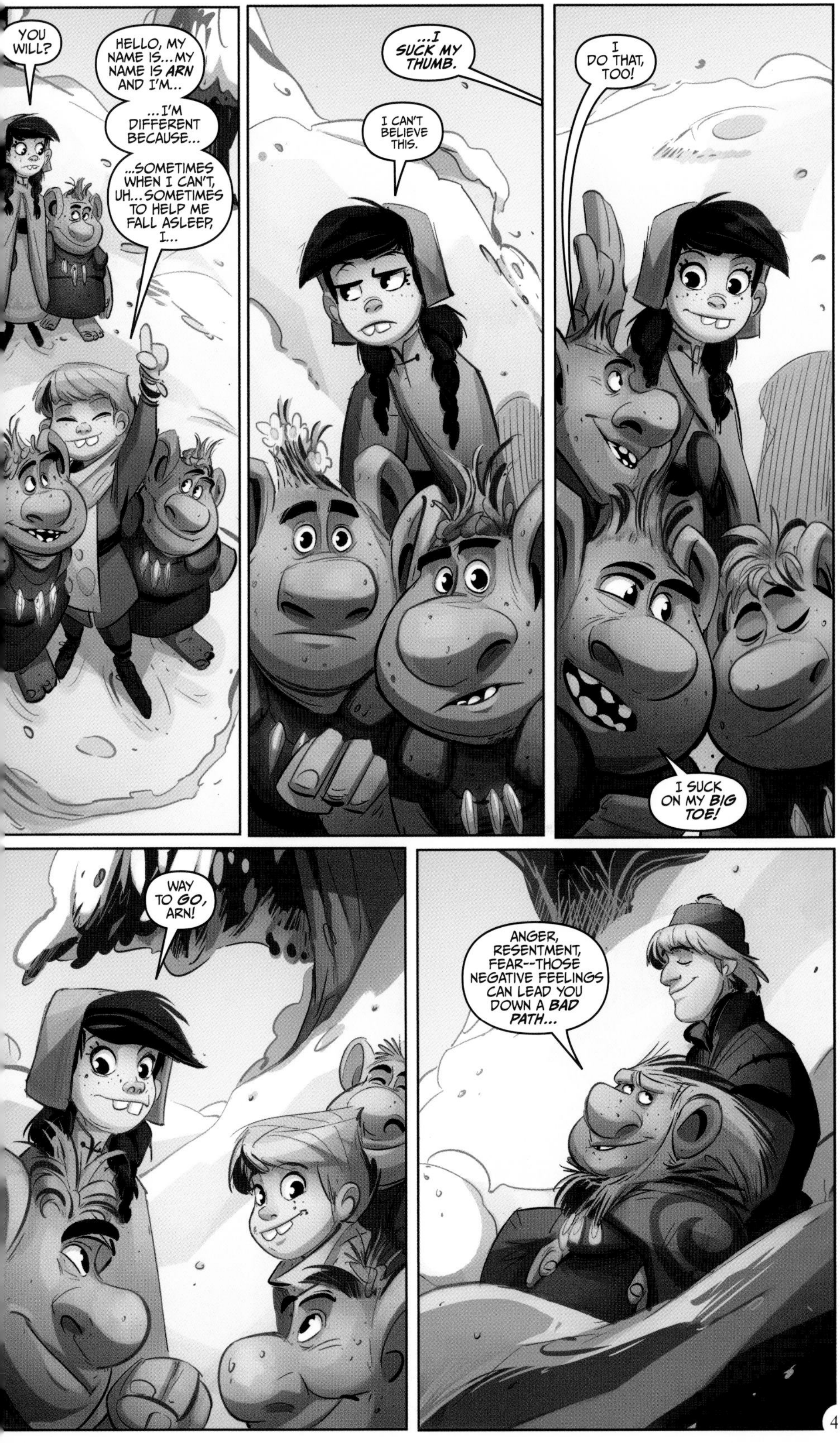
YOU WILL?
HELLO, MY NAME IS...MY NAME IS ARN AND I'M...
...I'M DIFFERENT BECAUSE...
...SOMETIMES WHEN I CAN'T, UH...SOMETIMES TO HELP ME FALL ASLEEP, I...
...I SUCK MY THUMB.
I CAN'T BELIEVE THIS.
I DO THAT, TOO!
I SUCK ON MY BIG TOE!
WAY TO GO, ARN!
ANGER, RESENTMENT, FEAR--THOSE NEGATIVE FEELINGS CAN LEAD YOU DOWN A BAD PATH...

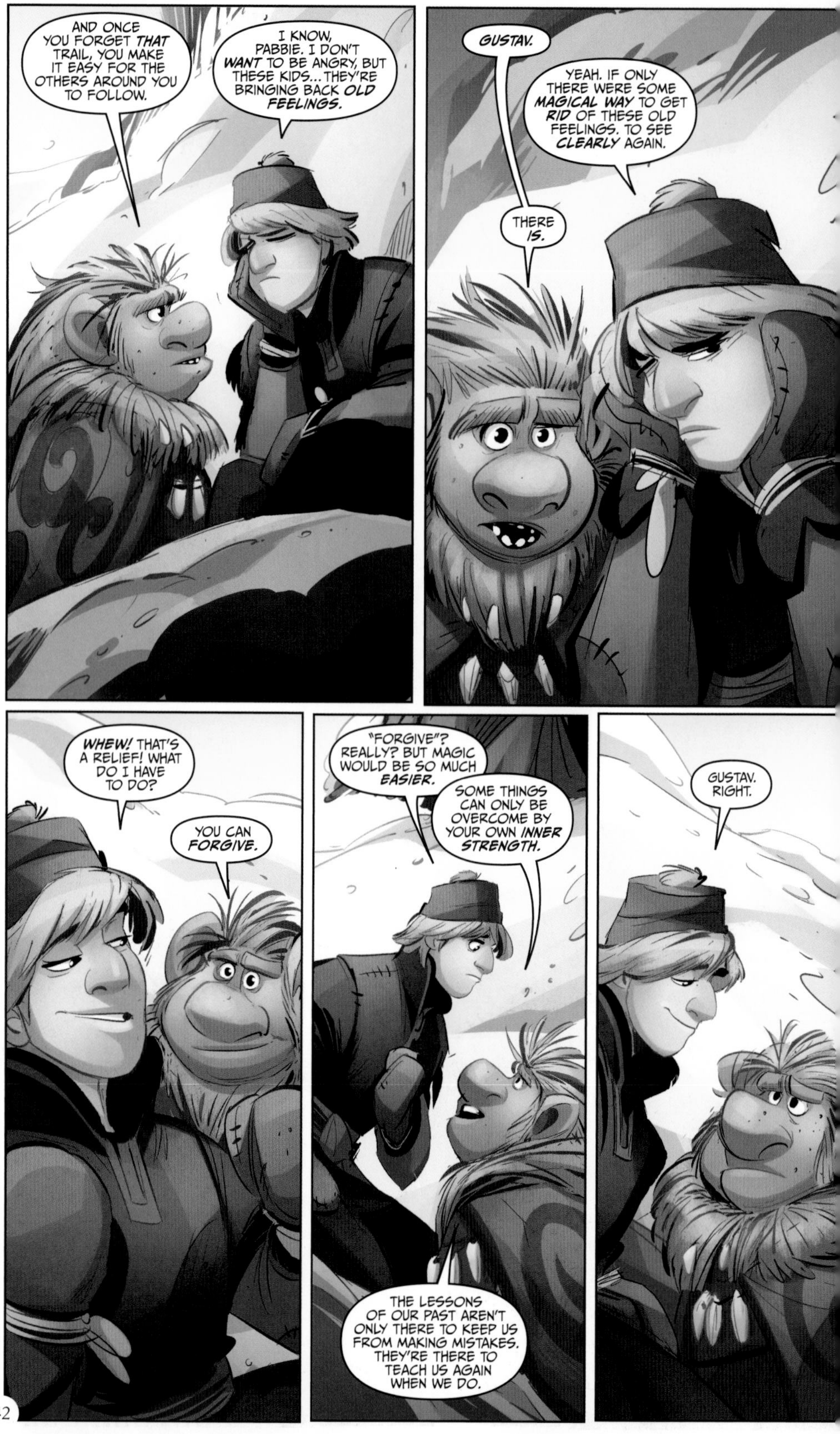

AND ONCE YOU FORGET THAT TRAIL, YOU MAKE IT EASY FOR THE OTHERS AROUND YOU TO FOLLOW.
I KNOW, PABBIE. I DON'T WANT TO BE ANGRY, BUT THESE KIDS... THEY'RE BRINGING BACK OLD FEELINGS.
GUSTAV.
YEAH. IF ONLY THERE WERE SOME MAGICAL WAY TO GET RID OF THESE OLD FEELINGS. TO SEE CLEARLY AGAIN.
THERE IS.
WHEW! THAT'S A RELIEF! WHAT DO I HAVE TO DO?
YOU CAN FORGIVE.
"FORGIVE"? REALLY? BUT MAGIC WOULD BE SO MUCH EASIER.
SOME THINGS CAN ONLY BE OVERCOME BY YOUR OWN INNER STRENGTH.
THE LESSONS OF OUR PAST AREN'T ONLY THERE TO KEEP US FROM MAKING MISTAKES. THEY'RE THERE TO TEACH US AGAIN WHEN WE DO.
GUSTAV. RIGHT.

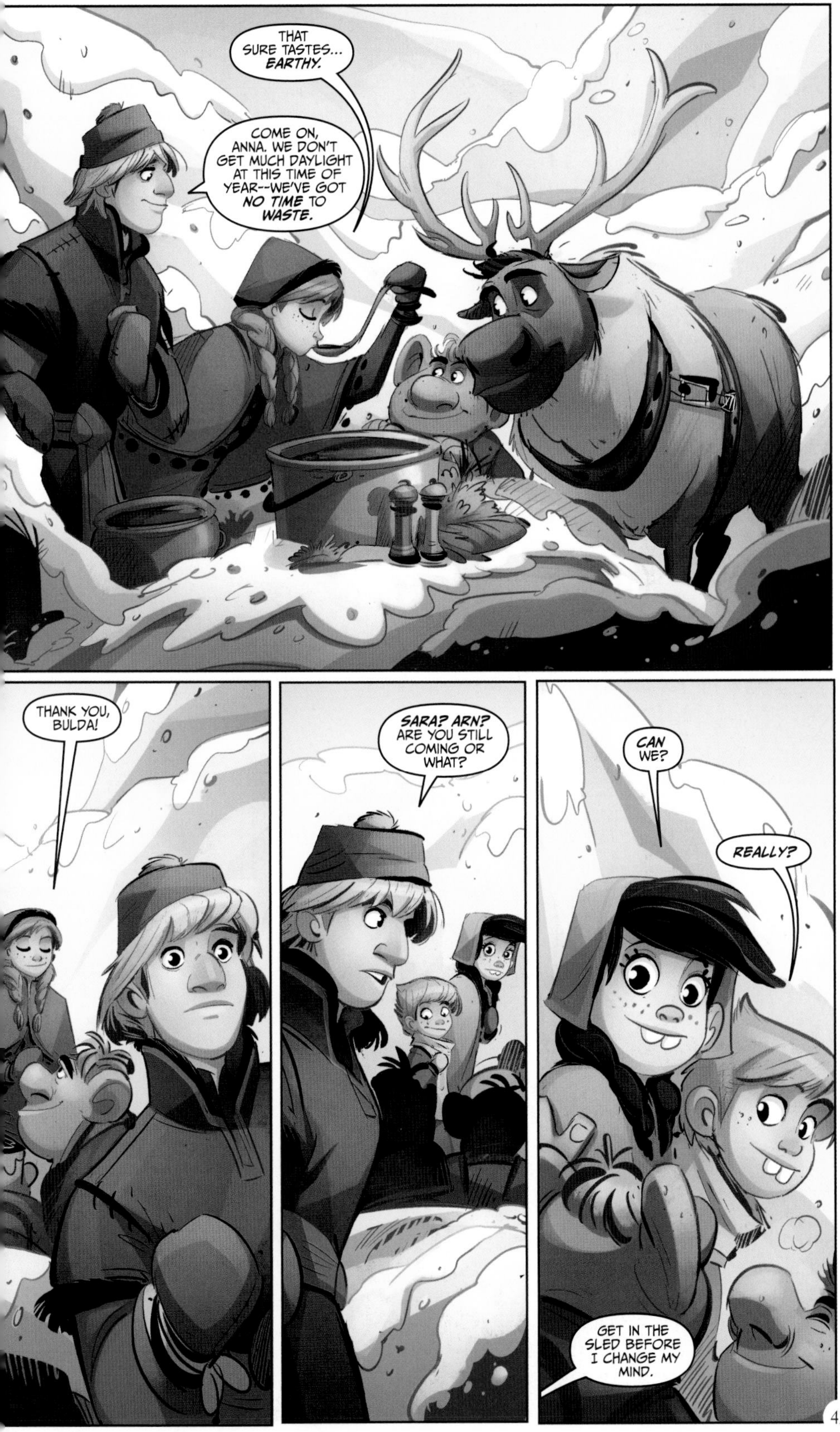
THAT SURE TASTES... EARTHY.
COME ON, ANNA. WE DON'T GET MUCH DAYLIGHT AT THIS TIME OF YEAR--WE'VE GOT NO TIME TO WASTE.
THANK YOU, BULDA!
SARA? ARN? ARE YOU STILL COMING OR WHAT?
CAN WE?
REALLY?
GET IN THE SLED BEFORE I CHANGE MY MIND.

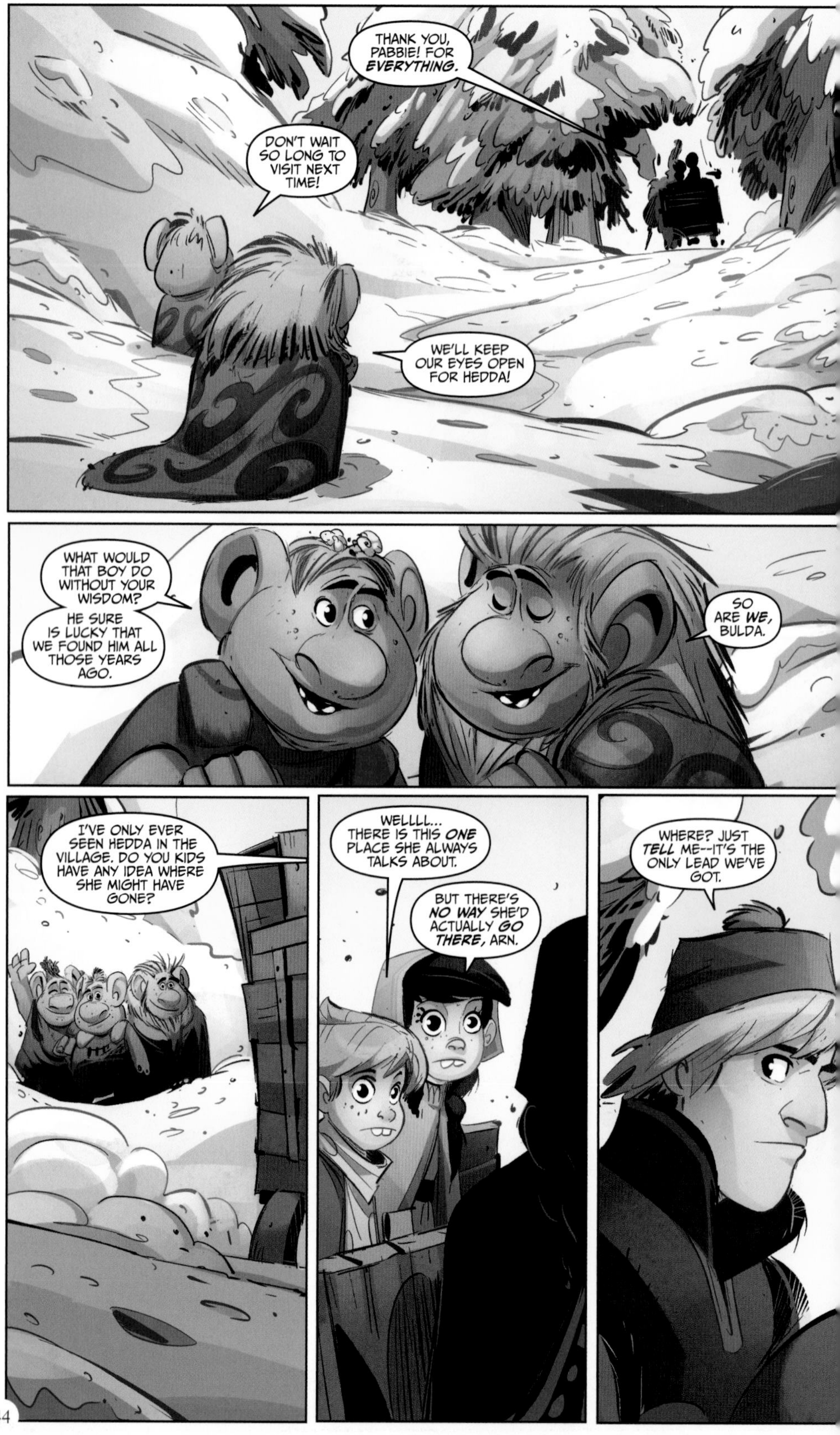
THANK YOU, PABBIE! FOR EVERYTHING.
DON'T WAIT SO LONG TO VISIT NEXT TIME!
WE'LL KEEP OUR EYES OPEN FOR HEDDA!
WHAT WOULD THAT BOY DO WITHOUT YOUR WISDOM?
HE SURE IS LUCKY THAT WE FOUND HIM ALL THOSE YEARS AGO.
SO ARE WE, BULDA.
I'VE ONLY EVER SEEN HEDDA IN THE VILLAGE. DO YOU KIDS HAVE ANY IDEA WHERE SHE MIGHT HAVE GONE?
WELLLL... THERE IS THIS ONE PLACE SHE ALWAYS TALKS ABOUT.
BUT THERE'S NO WAY SHE'D ACTUALLY GO THERE, ARN.
WHERE? JUST TELL ME--IT'S THE ONLY LEAD WE'VE GOT.

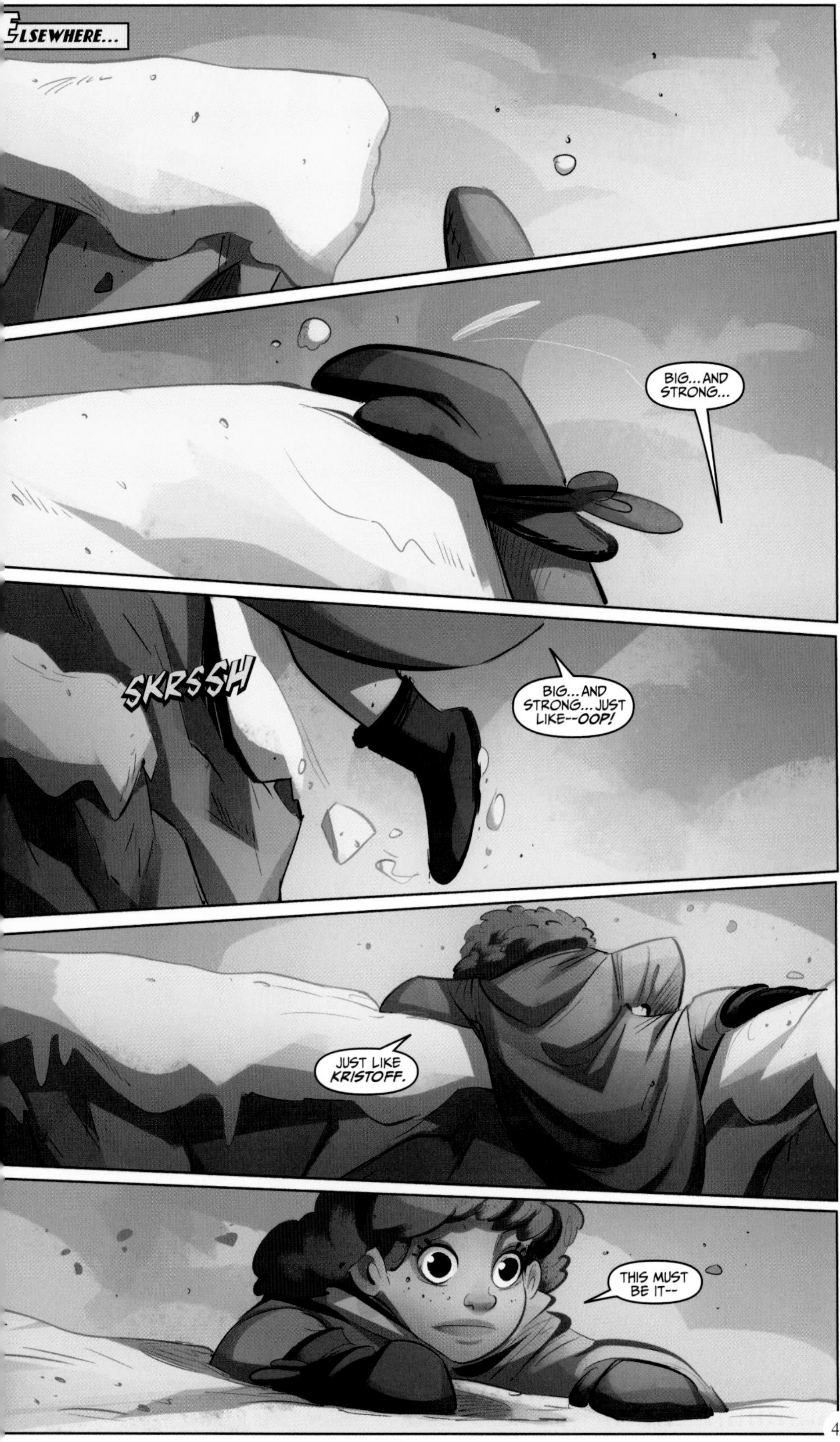

ELSEWHERE...
BIG...AND STRONG...
SKRSSH
BIG...AND STRONG...JUST LIKE--OOP!
JUST LIKE KRISTOFF.
THIS MUST BE IT--

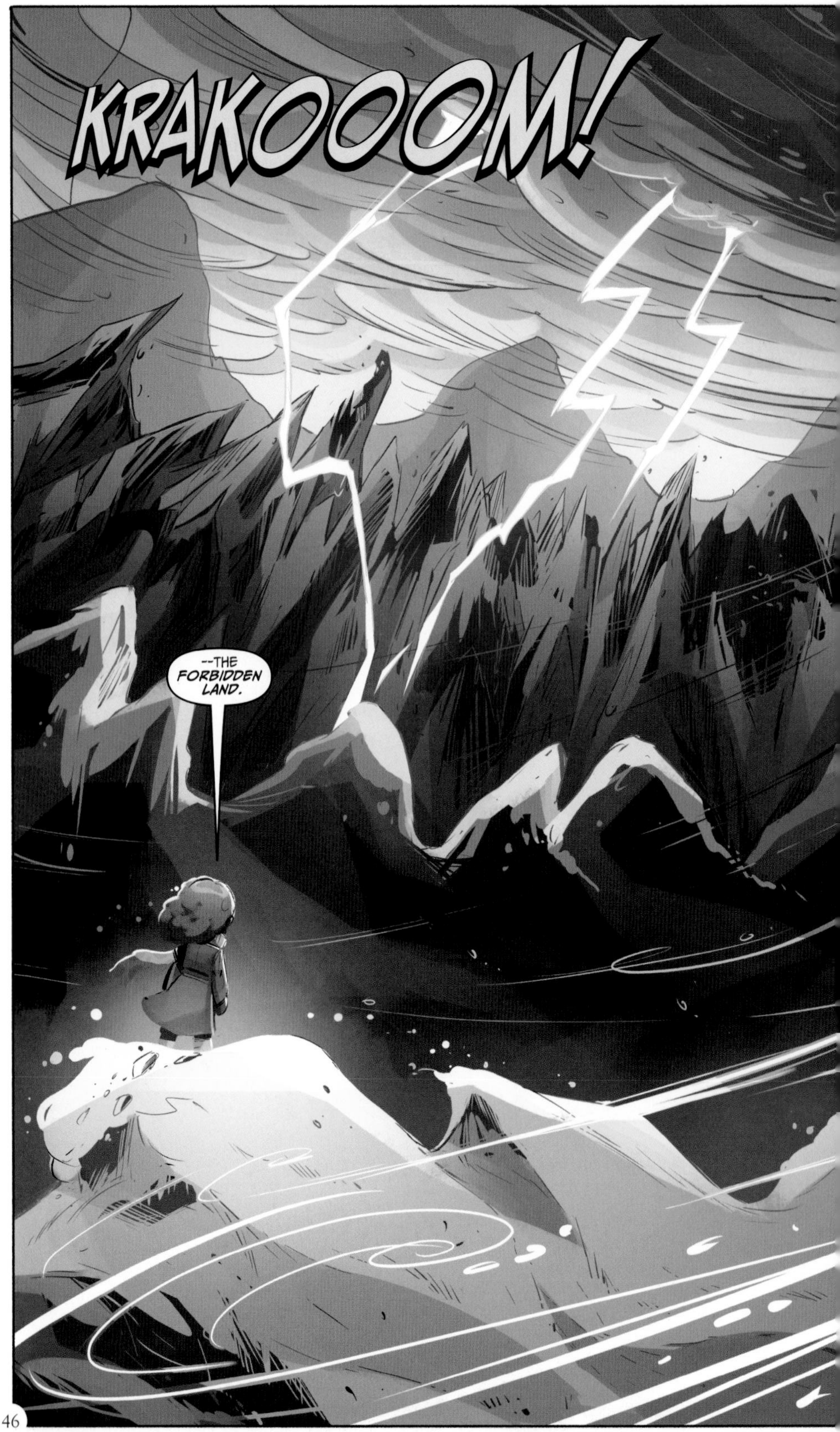
KRAKOOOM!
--THE FORBIDDEN LAND.

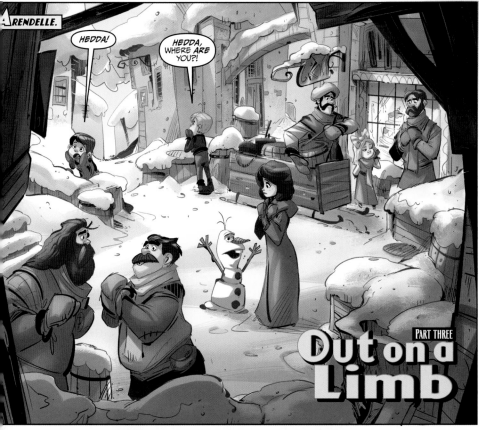

HEDDA!

HEDDA, WHERE *ARE* YOU?!

PART THREE
Out on a Limb

SHE LIKES TO EXPLORE... AND SHE HAS A GREAT IMAGINATION... SHE'S *FUNNY*...

HEDDA SOUNDS LIKE A GOOD FRIEND, OLAF... BUT WHAT I MEANT WAS WHAT DOES SHE *LOOK* LIKE?

IS THIS HEDDA A *FRIEND* OF YOURS?

FRIEND? NOT ANYMORE! I LET HER BORROW A BOW FOR HER HAIR AND SHE RUINED IT!

SHE WAS ON HER WAY TO THE CASTLE FOR A DINNER AND THAT'S THE LAST ANYONE'S SEEN OF HER.

I KNOW SHE WANDERS, BUT YOU SAY SHE'S BEEN MISSING *ALL NIGHT?* I'M SORRY, JON.

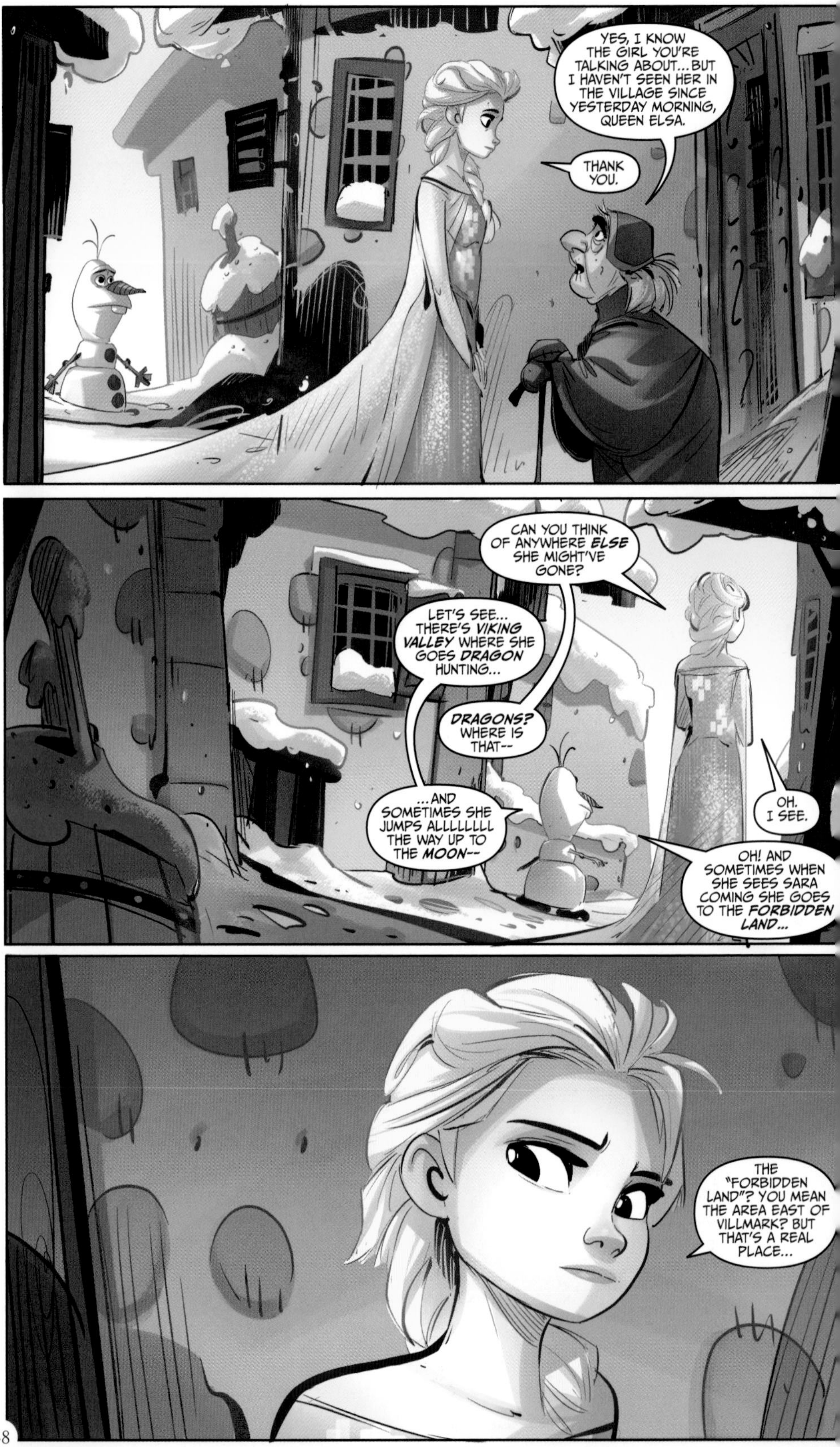
YES, I KNOW THE GIRL YOU'RE TALKING ABOUT... BUT I HAVEN'T SEEN HER IN THE VILLAGE SINCE YESTERDAY MORNING, QUEEN ELSA.
THANK YOU.
CAN YOU THINK OF ANYWHERE *ELSE* SHE MIGHT'VE GONE?
LET'S SEE... THERE'S *VIKING VALLEY* WHERE SHE GOES *DRAGON* HUNTING...
DRAGONS? WHERE IS THAT--
...AND SOMETIMES SHE JUMPS ALLLLLLLL THE WAY UP TO THE *MOON*--
OH. I SEE.
OH! AND SOMETIMES WHEN SHE SEES SARA COMING SHE GOES TO THE *FORBIDDEN LAND*...
THE "FORBIDDEN LAND"? YOU MEAN THE AREA EAST OF VILLMARK? BUT THAT'S A REAL PLACE...

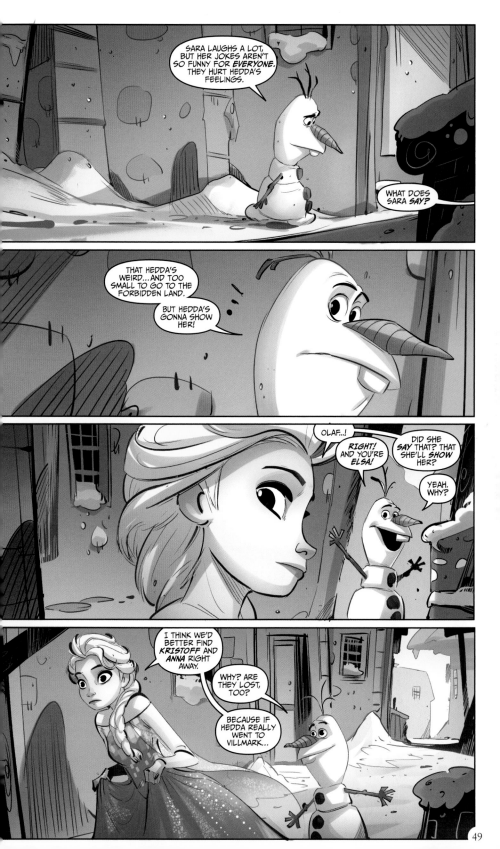

SARA LAUGHS A LOT, BUT HER JOKES AREN'T SO FUNNY FOR *EVERYONE*. THEY HURT HEDDA'S FEELINGS.

WHAT DOES SARA *SAY*?

THAT HEDDA'S WEIRD...AND TOO SMALL TO GO TO THE FORBIDDEN LAND.

BUT HEDDA'S GONNA SHOW HER!

OLAF...!

RIGHT! AND YOU'RE ELSA!

DID SHE SAY THAT? THAT SHE'LL *SHOW* HER?

YEAH. WHY?

I THINK WE'D BETTER FIND *KRISTOFF* AND *ANNA* RIGHT AWAY.

WHY? ARE THEY LOST, TOO?

BECAUSE IF HEDDA REALLY WENT TO VILLMARK...

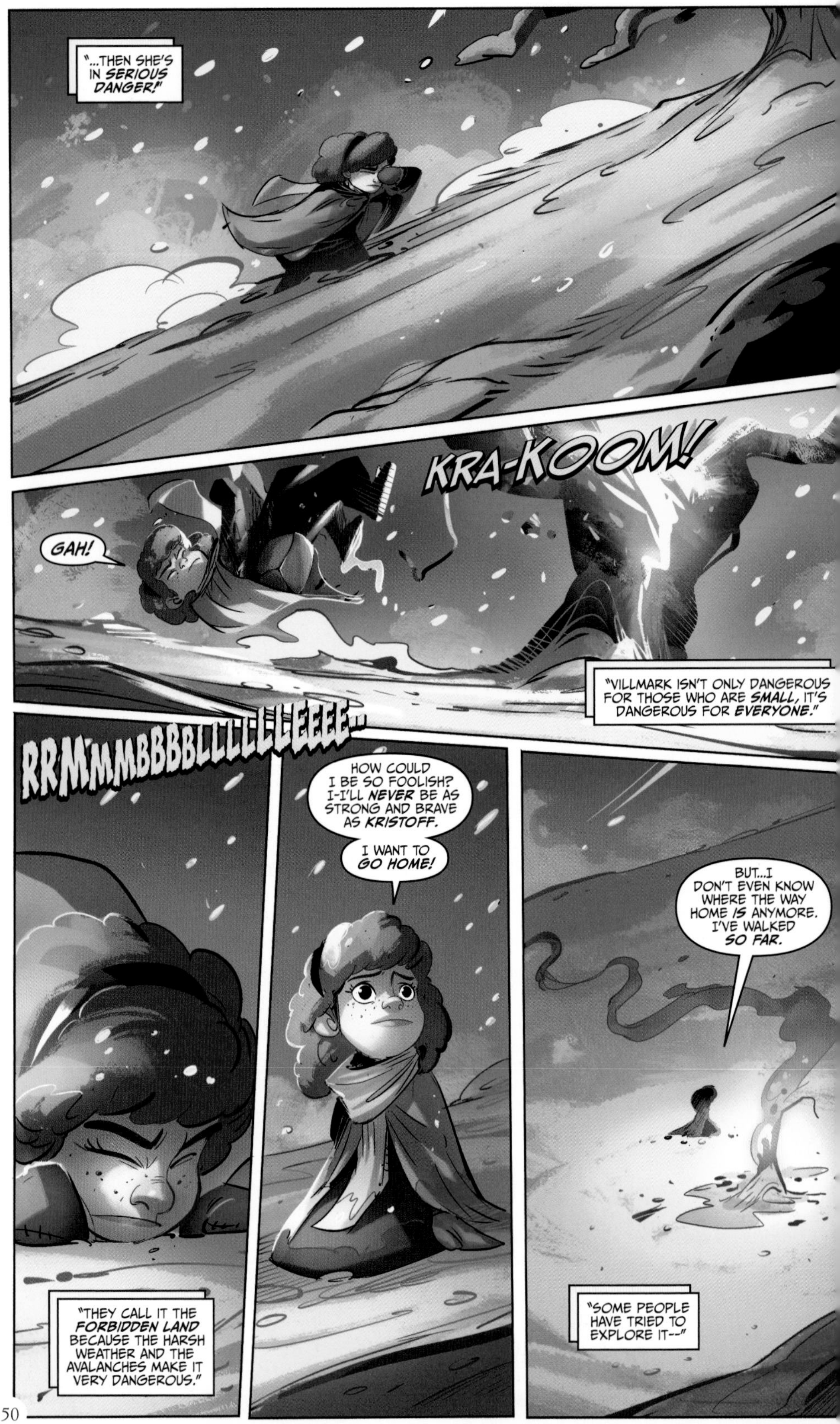

"...THEN SHE'S IN SERIOUS DANGER!"
KRA-KOOM!
GAH!
"VILLMARK ISN'T ONLY DANGEROUS FOR THOSE WHO ARE SMALL, IT'S DANGEROUS FOR EVERYONE."
RRMMMBBBLLLLLLEEEE...
HOW COULD I BE SO FOOLISH? I-I'LL NEVER BE AS STRONG AND BRAVE AS KRISTOFF.
I WANT TO GO HOME!
BUT...I DON'T EVEN KNOW WHERE THE WAY HOME IS ANYMORE. I'VE WALKED SO FAR.
"THEY CALL IT THE FORBIDDEN LAND BECAUSE THE HARSH WEATHER AND THE AVALANCHES MAKE IT VERY DANGEROUS."
"SOME PEOPLE HAVE TRIED TO EXPLORE IT--"

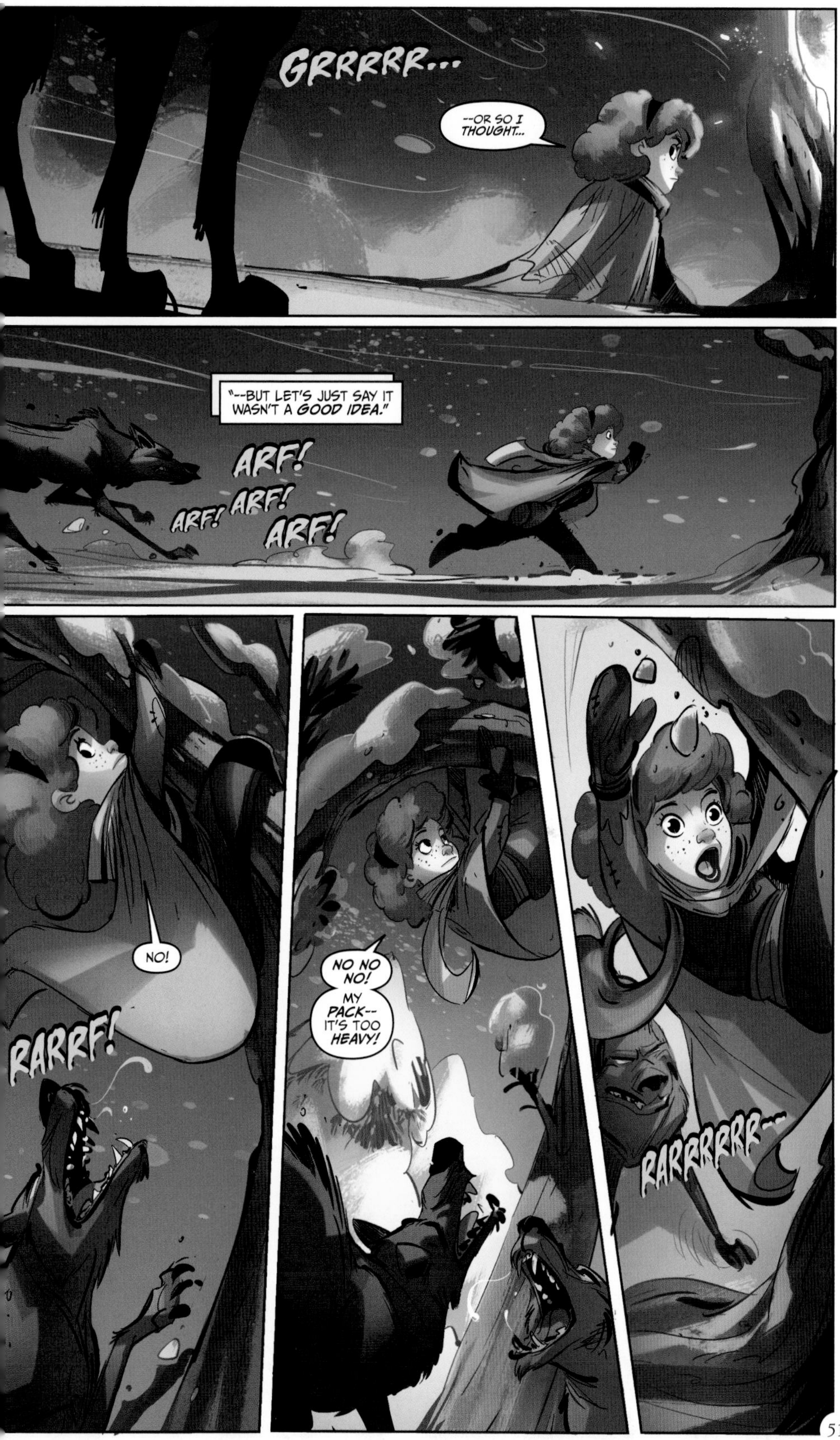
GRRRRR...
--OR SO I THOUGHT...
"--BUT LET'S JUST SAY IT WASN'T A GOOD IDEA."
ARF!
ARF! ARF!
ARF!
NO!
RARRF!
NO NO NO!
MY PACK-- IT'S TOO HEAVY!
RARRRRRR--

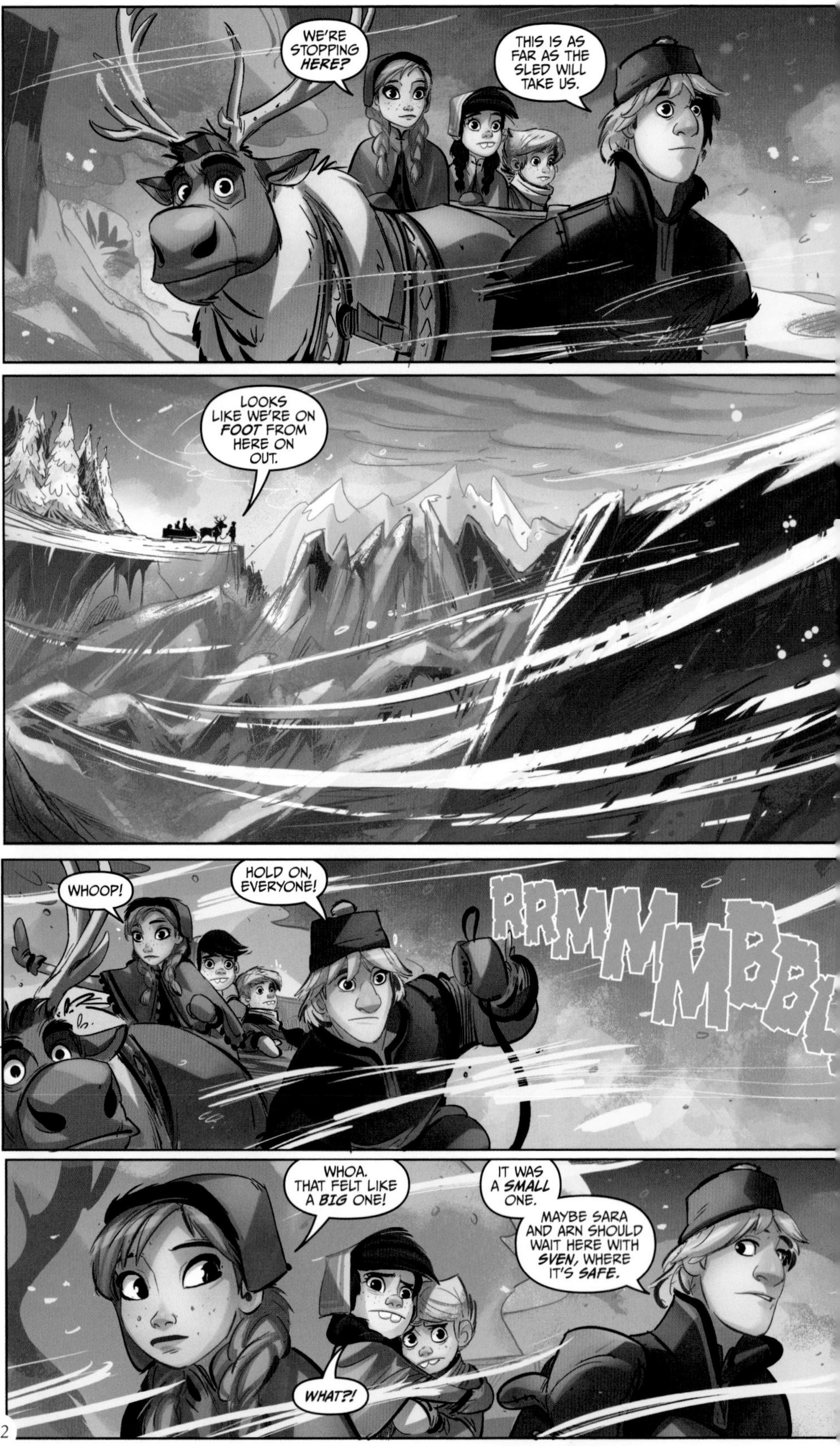
WE'RE STOPPING *HERE?*
THIS IS AS FAR AS THE SLED WILL TAKE US.
LOOKS LIKE WE'RE ON *FOOT* FROM HERE ON OUT.
WHOOP!
HOLD ON, EVERYONE!
RRMMMBBL
WHOA. THAT FELT LIKE A *BIG* ONE!
IT WAS A *SMALL* ONE.
MAYBE SARA AND ARN SHOULD WAIT HERE WITH *SVEN*, WHERE IT'S *SAFE*.
WHAT?!

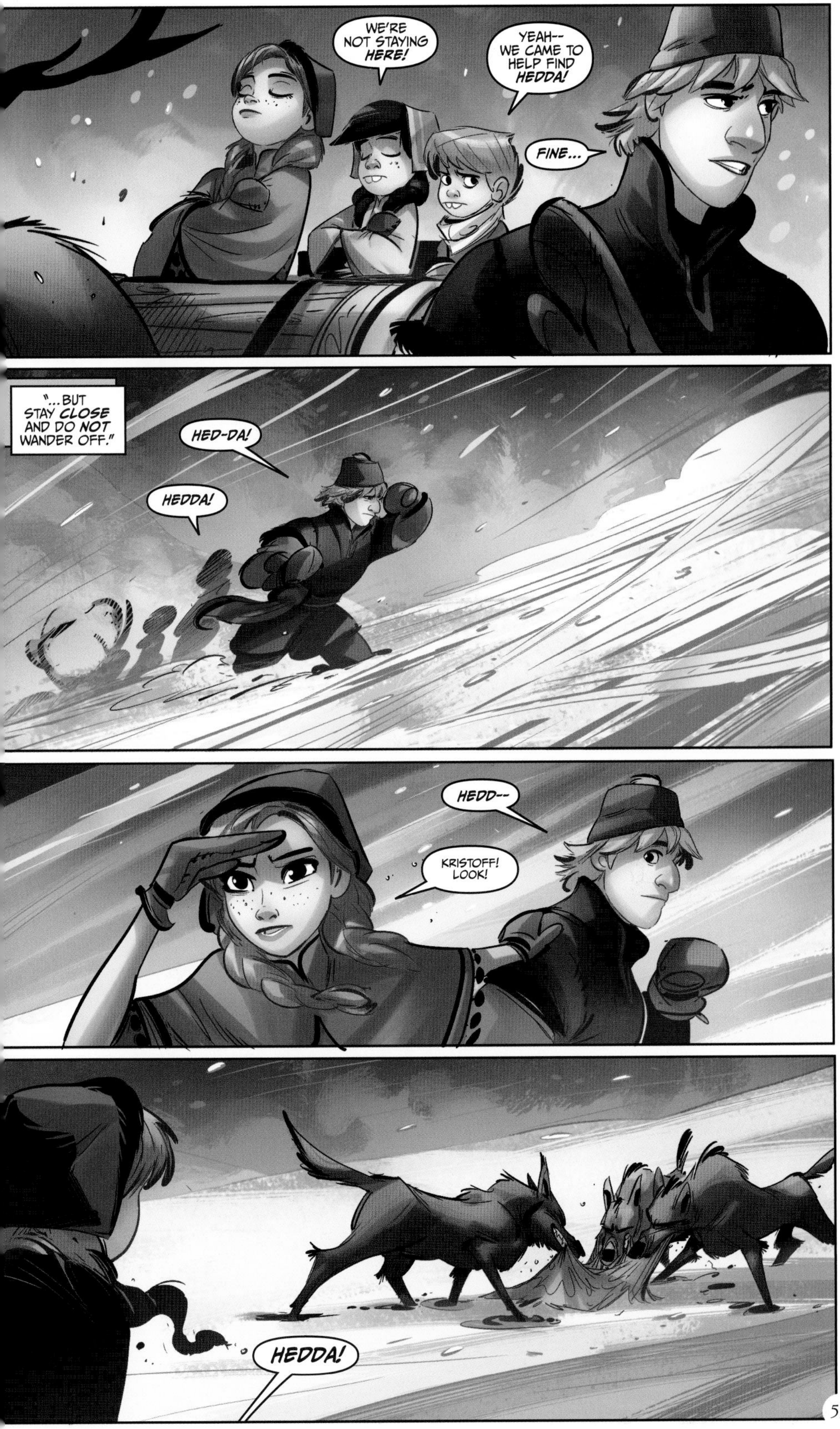
WE'RE NOT STAYING HERE!
YEAH-- WE CAME TO HELP FIND HEDDA!
FINE...
"...BUT STAY CLOSE AND DO NOT WANDER OFF."
HED-DA!
HEDDA!
HEDD--
KRISTOFF! LOOK!
HEDDA!

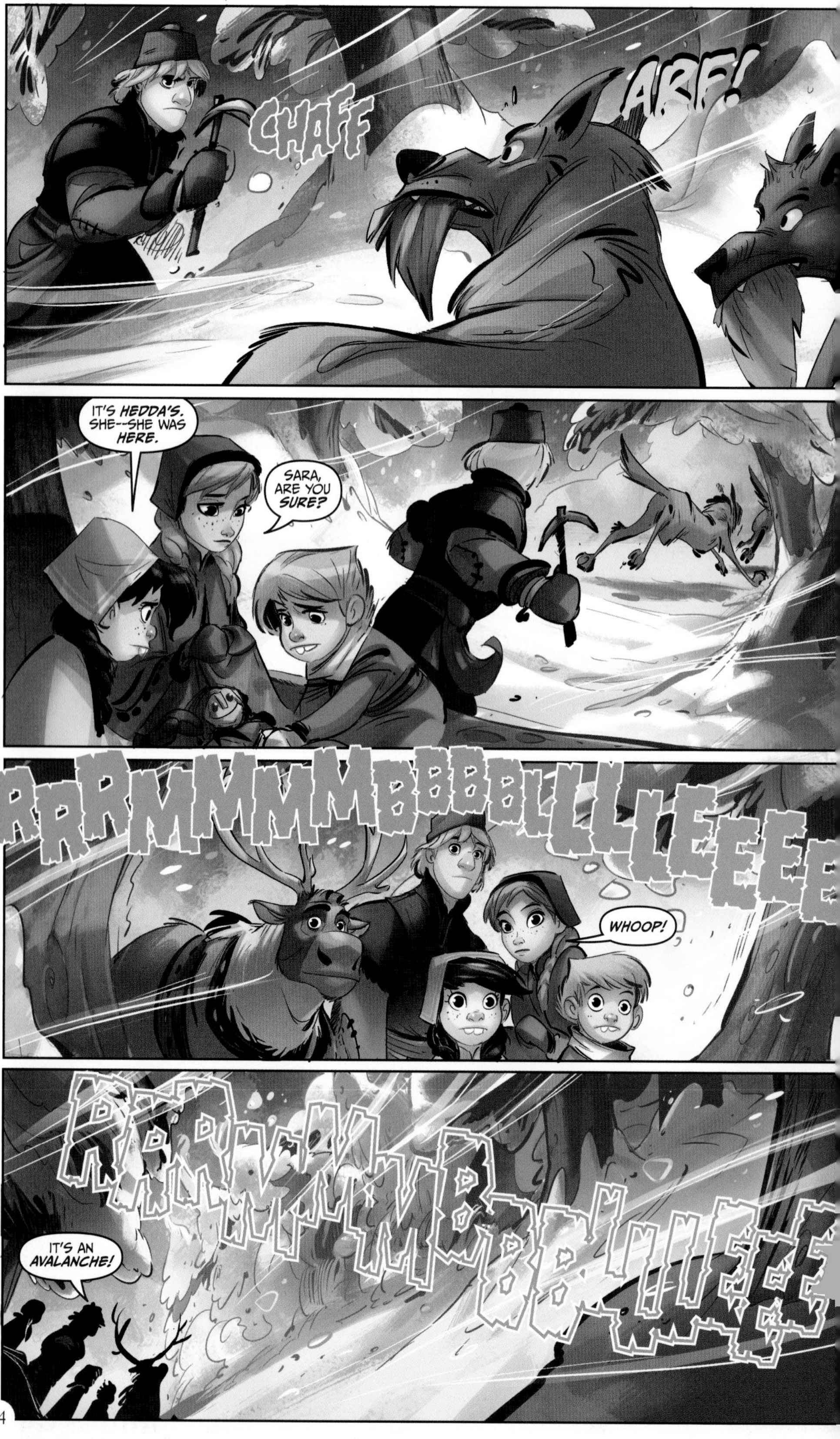
CHAFF
ARF!
IT'S HEDDA'S. SHE--SHE WAS HERE.
SARA, ARE YOU SURE?
RRRMMMMMBBBBLLLLEEEEE
WHOOP!
IT'S AN AVALANCHE!

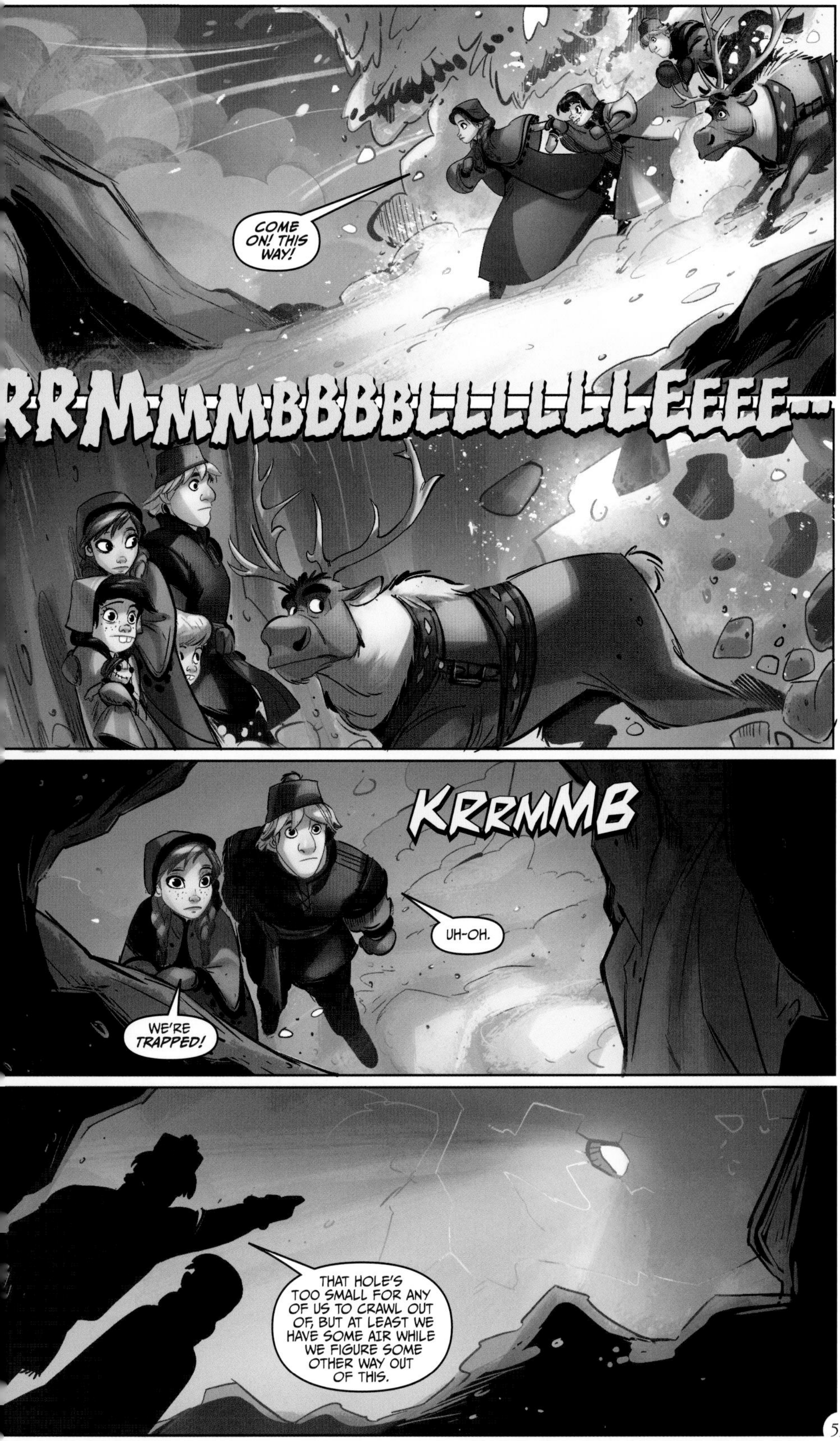

COME ON! THIS WAY!
RRMMMMBBBBLLLLLLEEEE...
KRRMMB
UH-OH.
WE'RE TRAPPED!
THAT HOLE'S TOO SMALL FOR ANY OF US TO CRAWL OUT OF, BUT AT LEAST WE HAVE SOME AIR WHILE WE FIGURE SOME OTHER WAY OUT OF THIS.

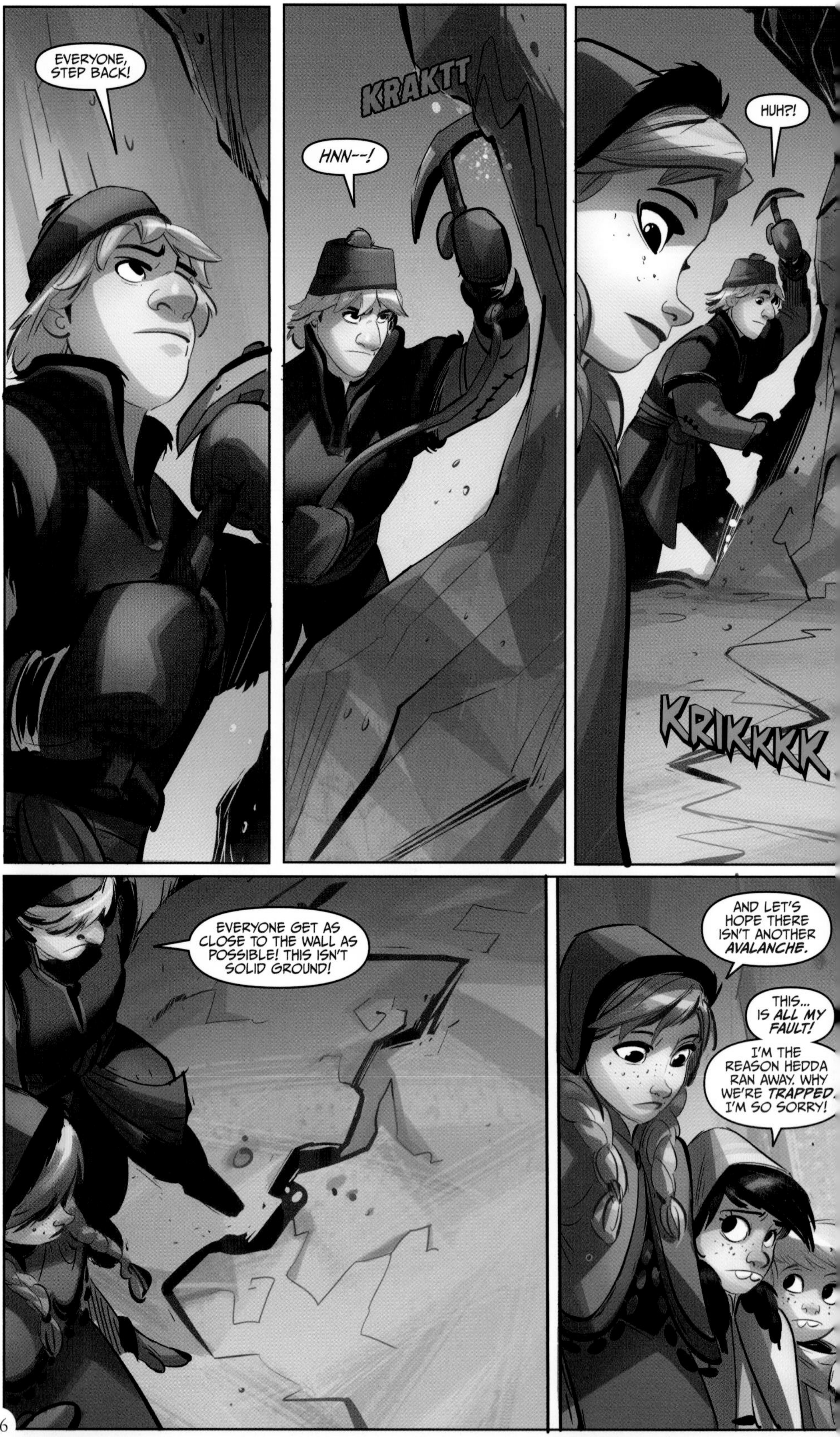
EVERYONE, STEP BACK!
KRAKTT
HNN--!
HUH?!
KRIKKKK
EVERYONE GET AS CLOSE TO THE WALL AS POSSIBLE! THIS ISN'T SOLID GROUND!
AND LET'S HOPE THERE ISN'T ANOTHER **AVALANCHE.**
THIS... IS **ALL MY FAULT!**
I'M THE REASON HEDDA RAN AWAY. WHY WE'RE **TRAPPED.** I'M SO SORRY!

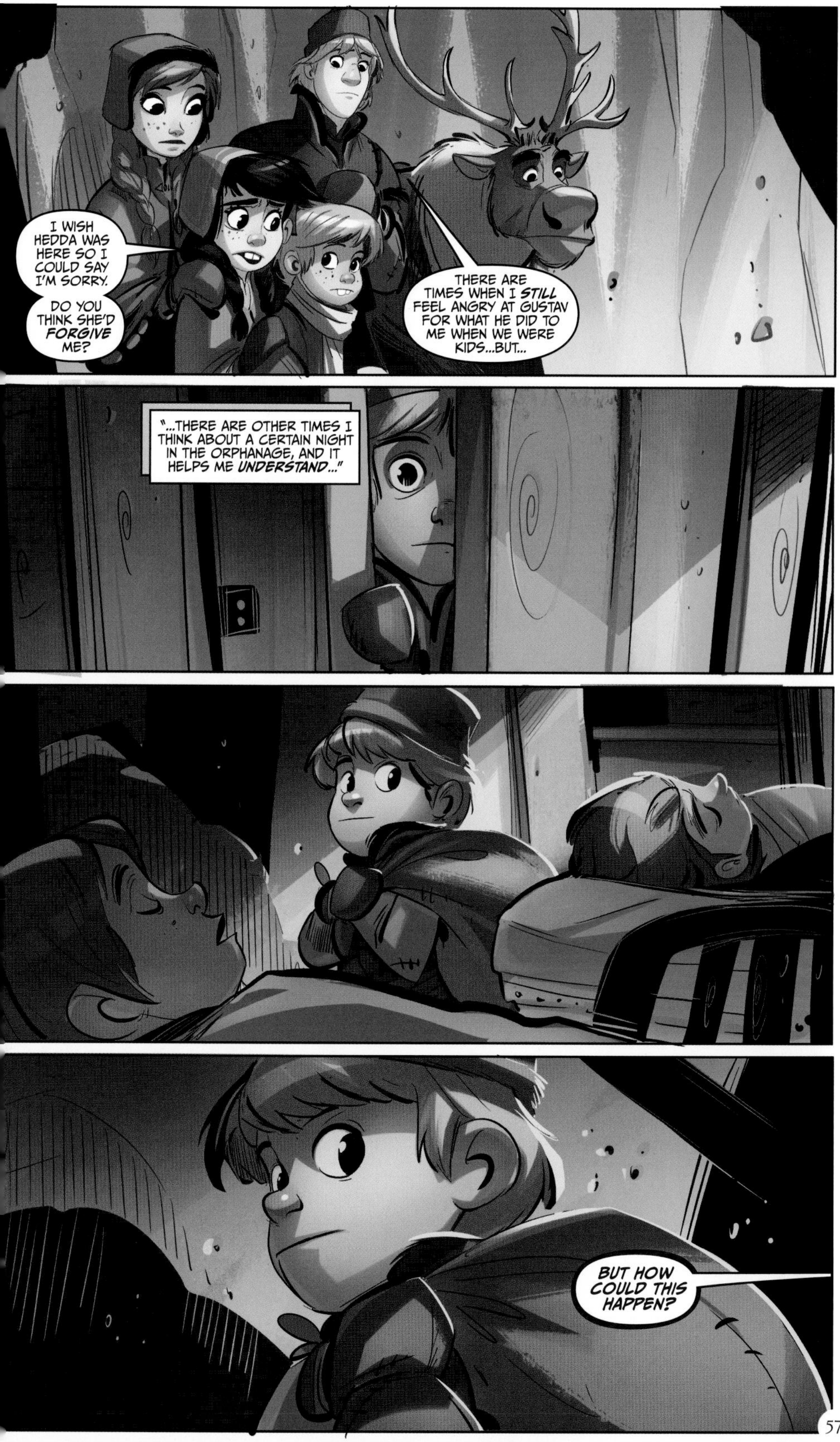
I WISH HEDDA WAS HERE SO I COULD SAY I'M SORRY.
DO YOU THINK SHE'D FORGIVE ME?
THERE ARE TIMES WHEN I STILL FEEL ANGRY AT GUSTAV FOR WHAT HE DID TO ME WHEN WE WERE KIDS...BUT...
"...THERE ARE OTHER TIMES I THINK ABOUT A CERTAIN NIGHT IN THE ORPHANAGE, AND IT HELPS ME UNDERSTAND..."
BUT HOW COULD THIS HAPPEN?

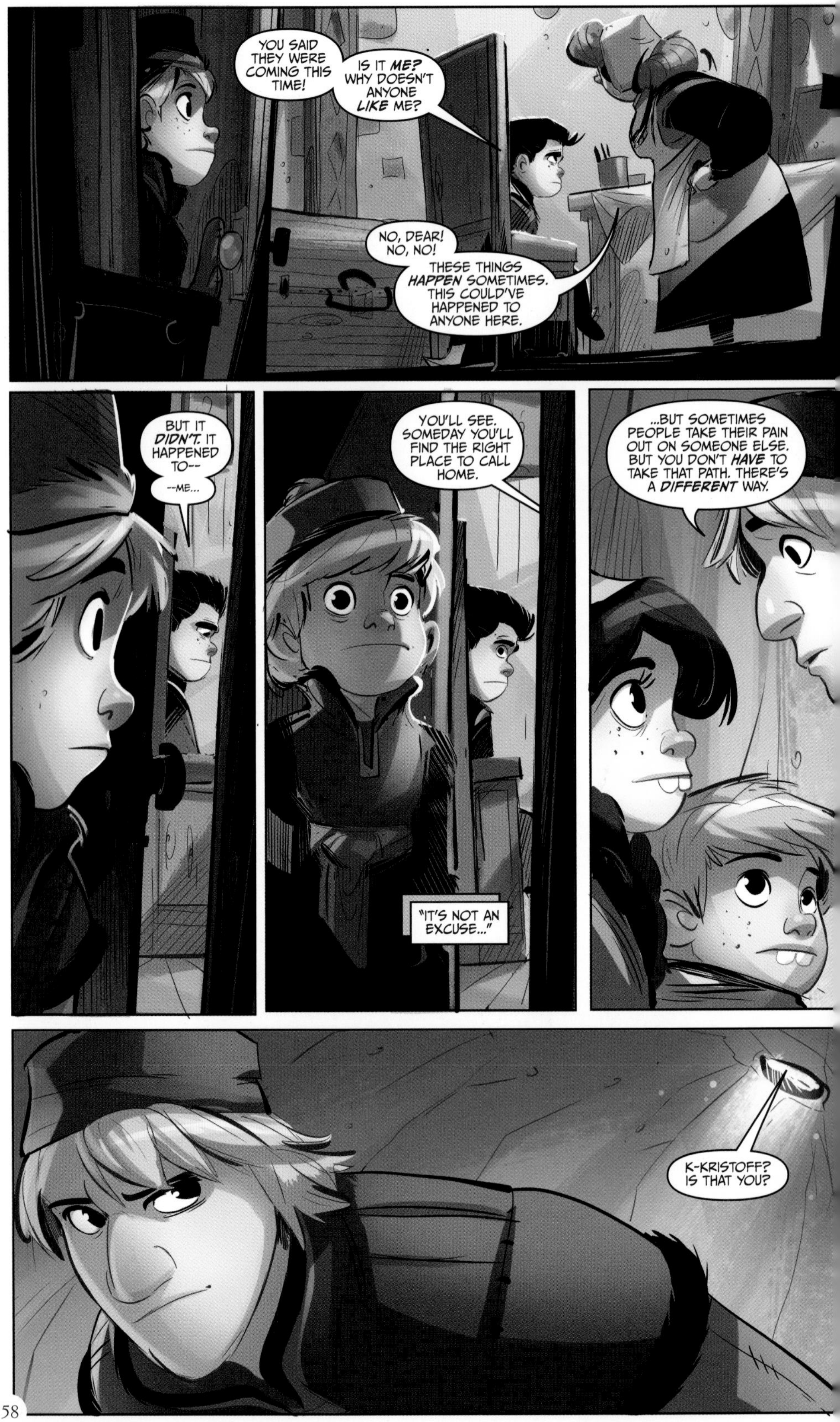

YOU SAID THEY WERE COMING THIS TIME!
IS IT *ME?* WHY DOESN'T ANYONE *LIKE* ME?
NO, DEAR! NO, NO!
THESE THINGS *HAPPEN* SOMETIMES. THIS COULD'VE HAPPENED TO ANYONE HERE.
BUT IT *DIDN'T.* IT HAPPENED TO--
--ME...
YOU'LL SEE. SOMEDAY YOU'LL FIND THE RIGHT PLACE TO CALL HOME.
"IT'S NOT AN EXCUSE..."
...BUT SOMETIMES PEOPLE TAKE THEIR PAIN OUT ON SOMEONE ELSE. BUT YOU DON'T *HAVE* TO TAKE THAT PATH. THERE'S A *DIFFERENT* WAY.
K-KRISTOFF? IS THAT YOU?

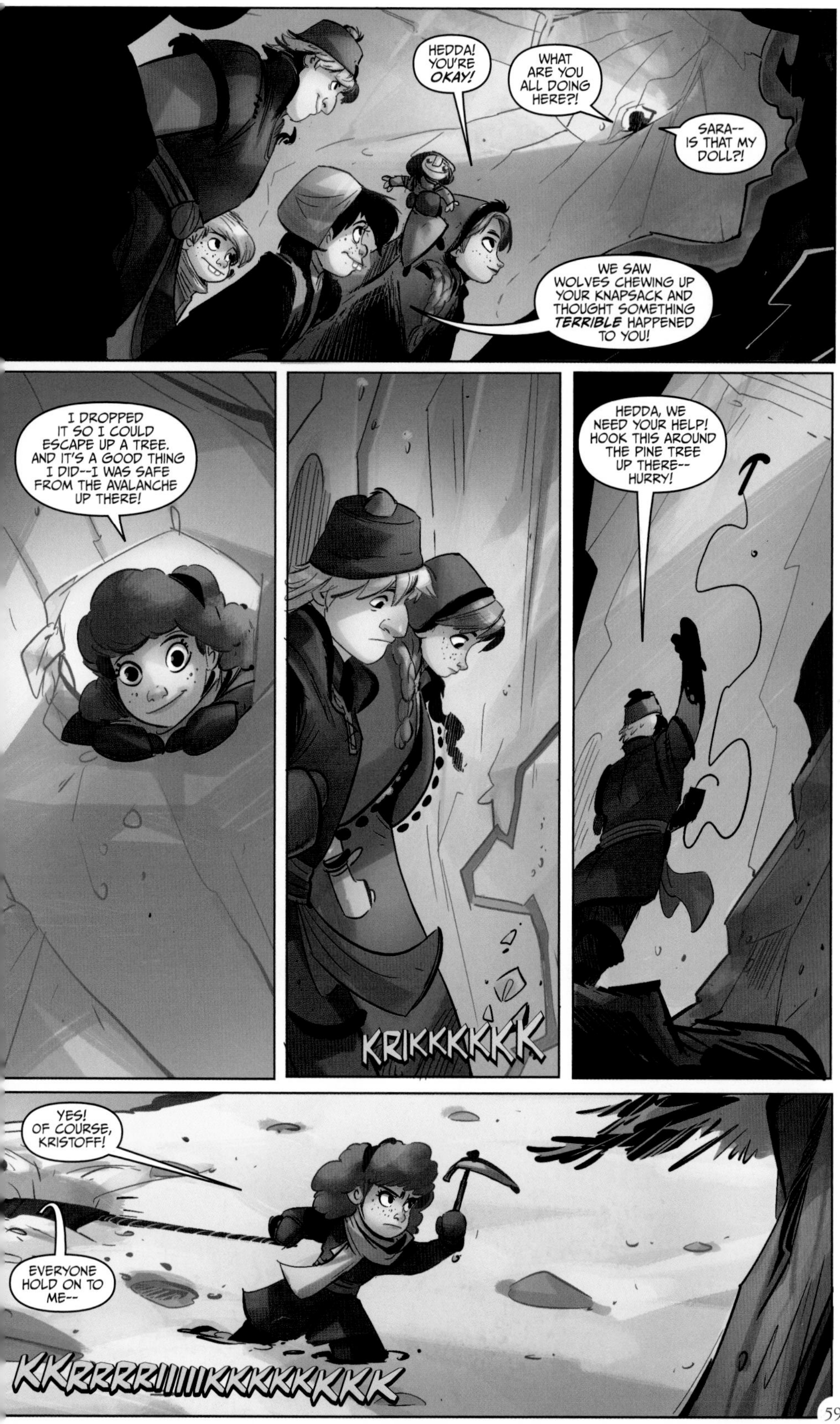
HEDDA! YOU'RE *OKAY!*
WHAT ARE YOU ALL DOING HERE?!
SARA-- IS THAT MY DOLL?!
WE SAW WOLVES CHEWING UP YOUR KNAPSACK AND THOUGHT SOMETHING *TERRIBLE* HAPPENED TO YOU!
I DROPPED IT SO I COULD ESCAPE UP A TREE. AND IT'S A GOOD THING I DID--I WAS SAFE FROM THE AVALANCHE UP THERE!
KRIKKKKKK
HEDDA, WE NEED YOUR HELP! HOOK THIS AROUND THE PINE TREE UP THERE-- HURRY!
YES! OF COURSE, KRISTOFF!
EVERYONE HOLD ON TO ME--
KKRRRRIIIIIKKKKKKKKK

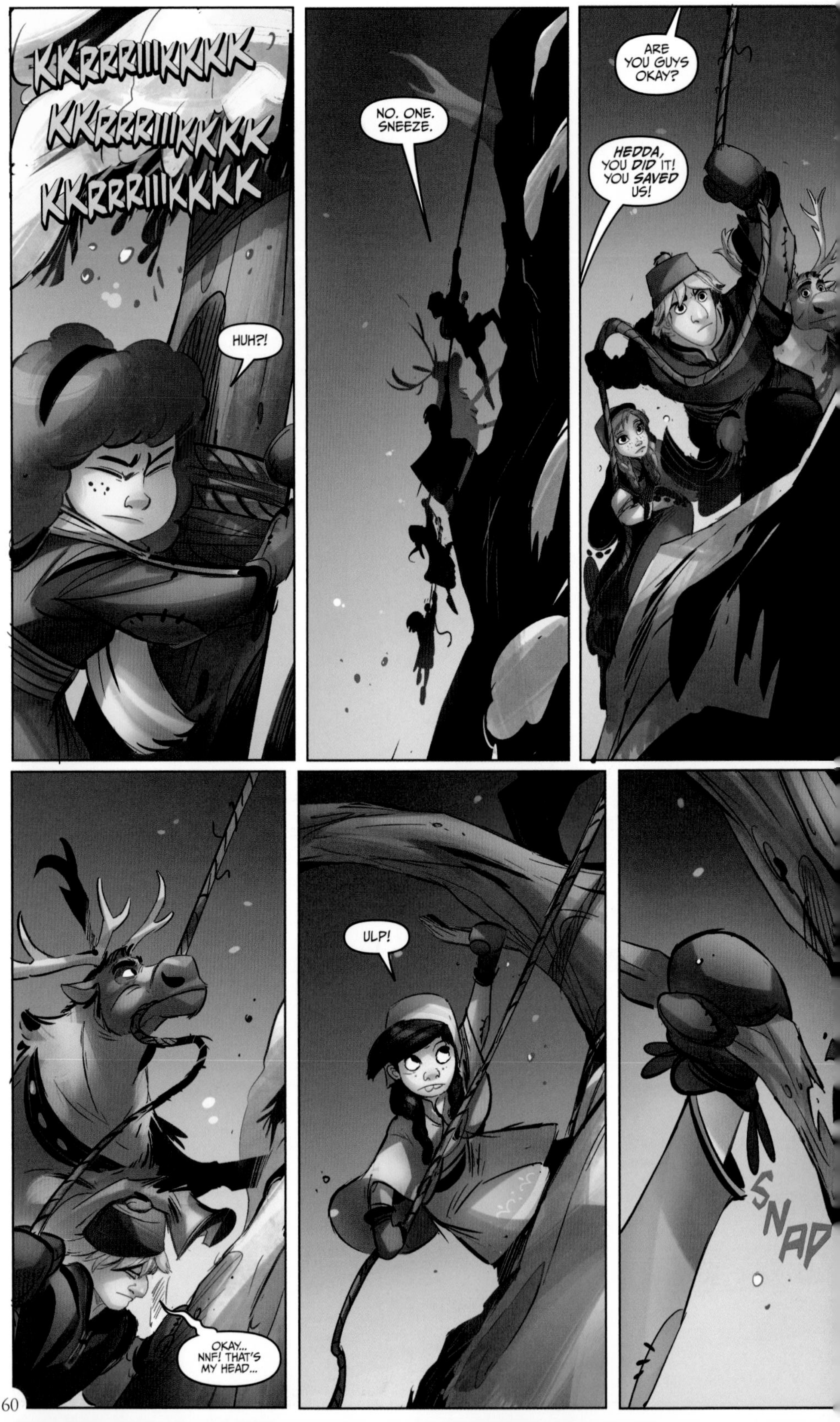
KKRRRIIIKKKK
KKRRRIIIKKKK
KKRRRIIIKKKK
HUH?!
NO. ONE. SNEEZE.
ARE YOU GUYS OKAY?
HEDDA, YOU DID IT! YOU SAVED US!
OKAY... NNF! THAT'S MY HEAD...
ULP!
SNAP

SARA!
SARA, HOLD ON TIGHT! I'M COMING!
OH NO, YOU'RE NOT! WE'RE TOO HEAVY FOR THE BRANCH!
SARA, YOU HAVE TO PULL YOURSELF CLOSER WHERE WE CAN REACH YOU!
I--I CAN'T! I'M SCARED!
H-HEDDA... I'M SORRY.
I FEEL LIKE I HAVE TO BE A CERTAIN WAY AND LOOK A CERTAIN WAY JUST SO PEOPLE WILL LIKE ME...
...BUT IT DOESN'T WORK. BUT YOU...
SARA, STAY CALM. THE BRANCH--
...YOU DON'T CARE WHAT ANYONE THINKS.
YOU DO WHAT YOU WANT TO DO.
I GUESS I WAS SO MEAN TO YOU BECAUSE...I WAS JEALOUS.
WILL YOU FORGIVE ME?

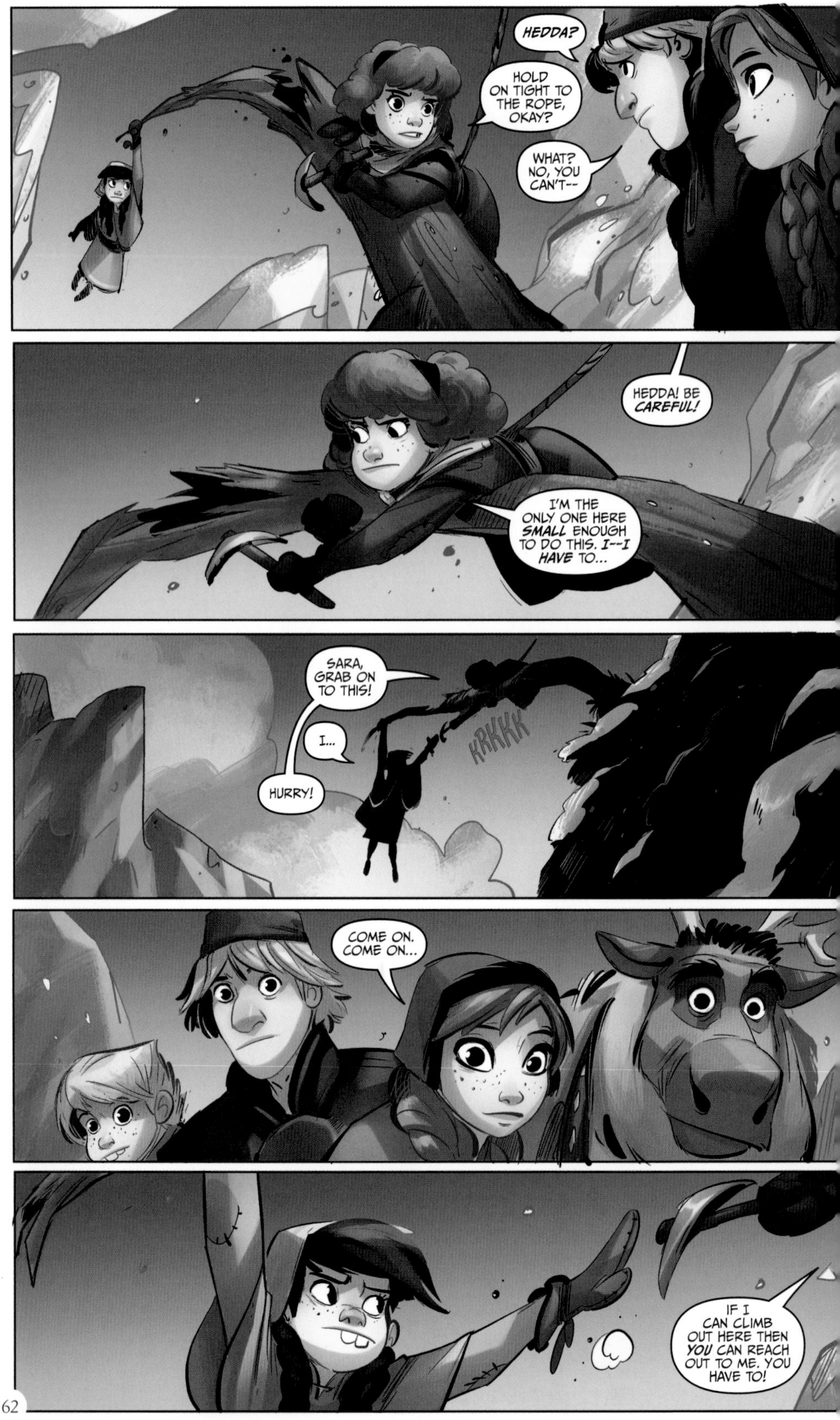
HEDDA?
HOLD ON TIGHT TO THE ROPE, OKAY?
WHAT? NO, YOU CAN'T--
HEDDA! BE CAREFUL!
I'M THE ONLY ONE HERE SMALL ENOUGH TO DO THIS. I--I HAVE TO...
SARA, GRAB ON TO THIS!
I...
HURRY!
KRKKK
COME ON. COME ON...
IF I CAN CLIMB OUT HERE THEN YOU CAN REACH OUT TO ME. YOU HAVE TO!

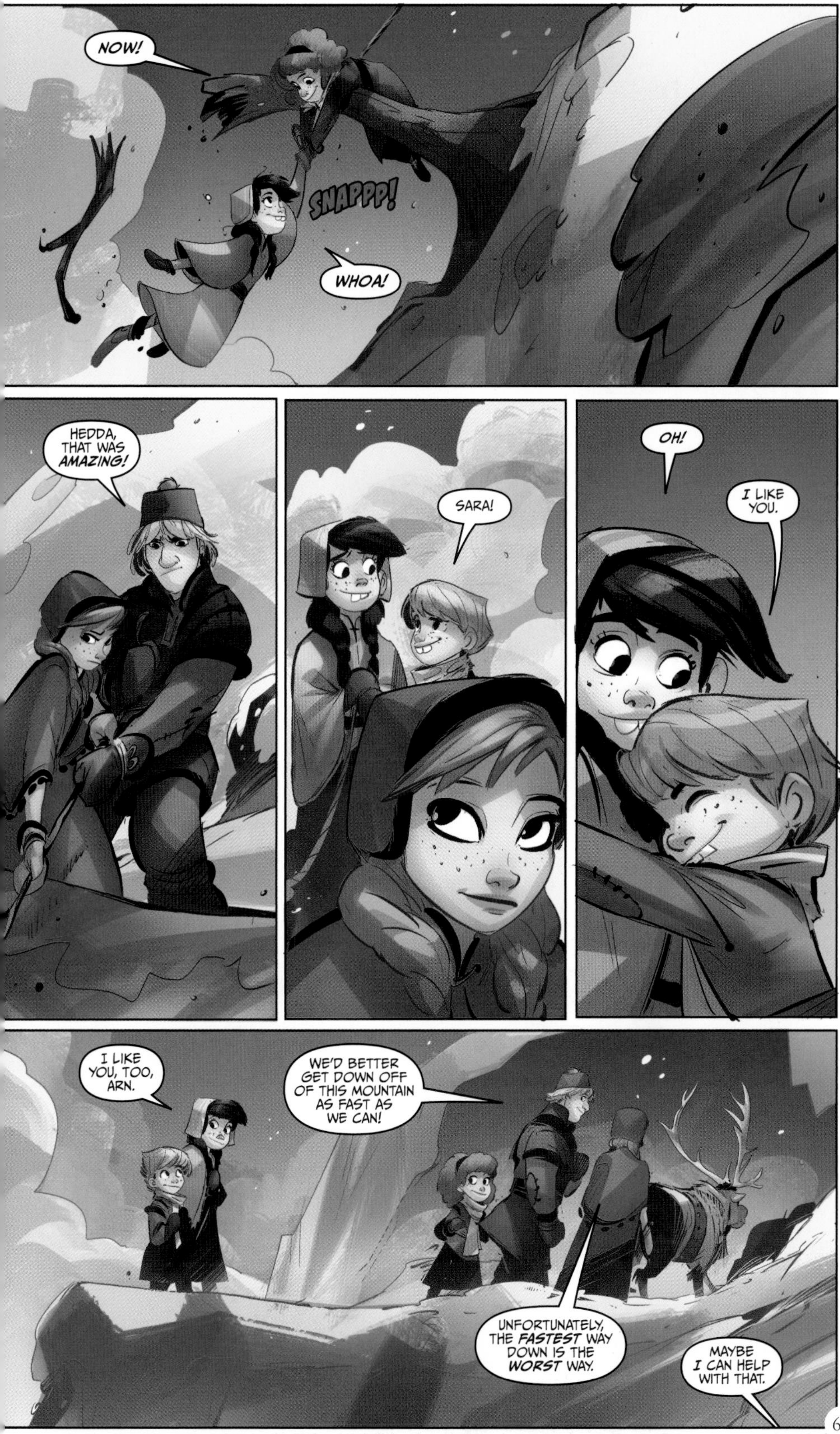
NOW!
SNAPPP!
WHOA!
HEDDA, THAT WAS AMAZING!
SARA!
OH!
I LIKE YOU.
I LIKE YOU, TOO, ARN.
WE'D BETTER GET DOWN OFF OF THIS MOUNTAIN AS FAST AS WE CAN!
UNFORTUNATELY, THE FASTEST WAY DOWN IS THE WORST WAY.
MAYBE I CAN HELP WITH THAT.

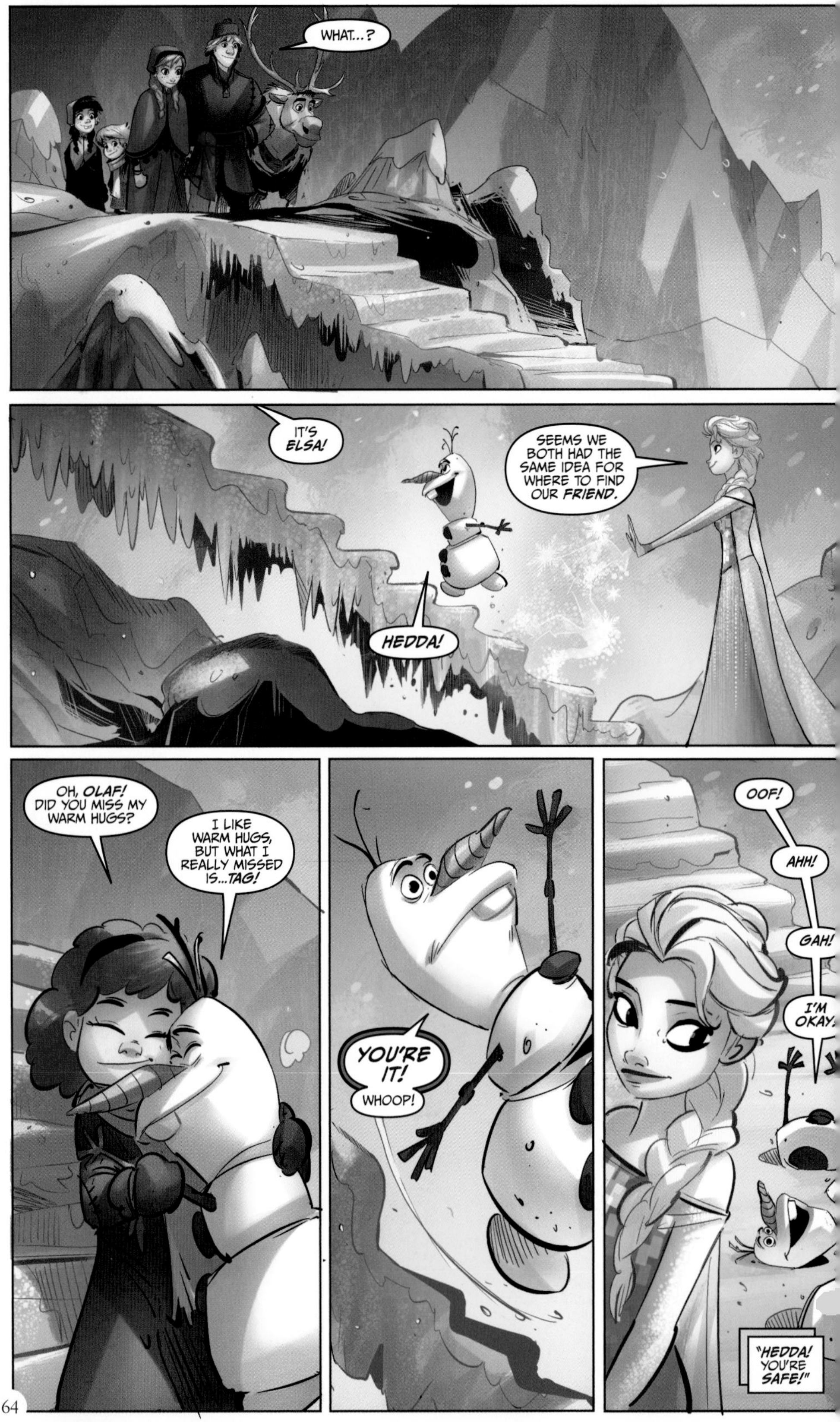
WHAT...?
IT'S ELSA!
SEEMS WE BOTH HAD THE SAME IDEA FOR WHERE TO FIND OUR FRIEND.
HEDDA!
OH, OLAF! DID YOU MISS MY WARM HUGS?
I LIKE WARM HUGS, BUT WHAT I REALLY MISSED IS...TAG!
YOU'RE IT!
WHOOP!
OOF!
AHH!
GAH!
I'M OKAY.
"HEDDA! YOU'RE SAFE!"

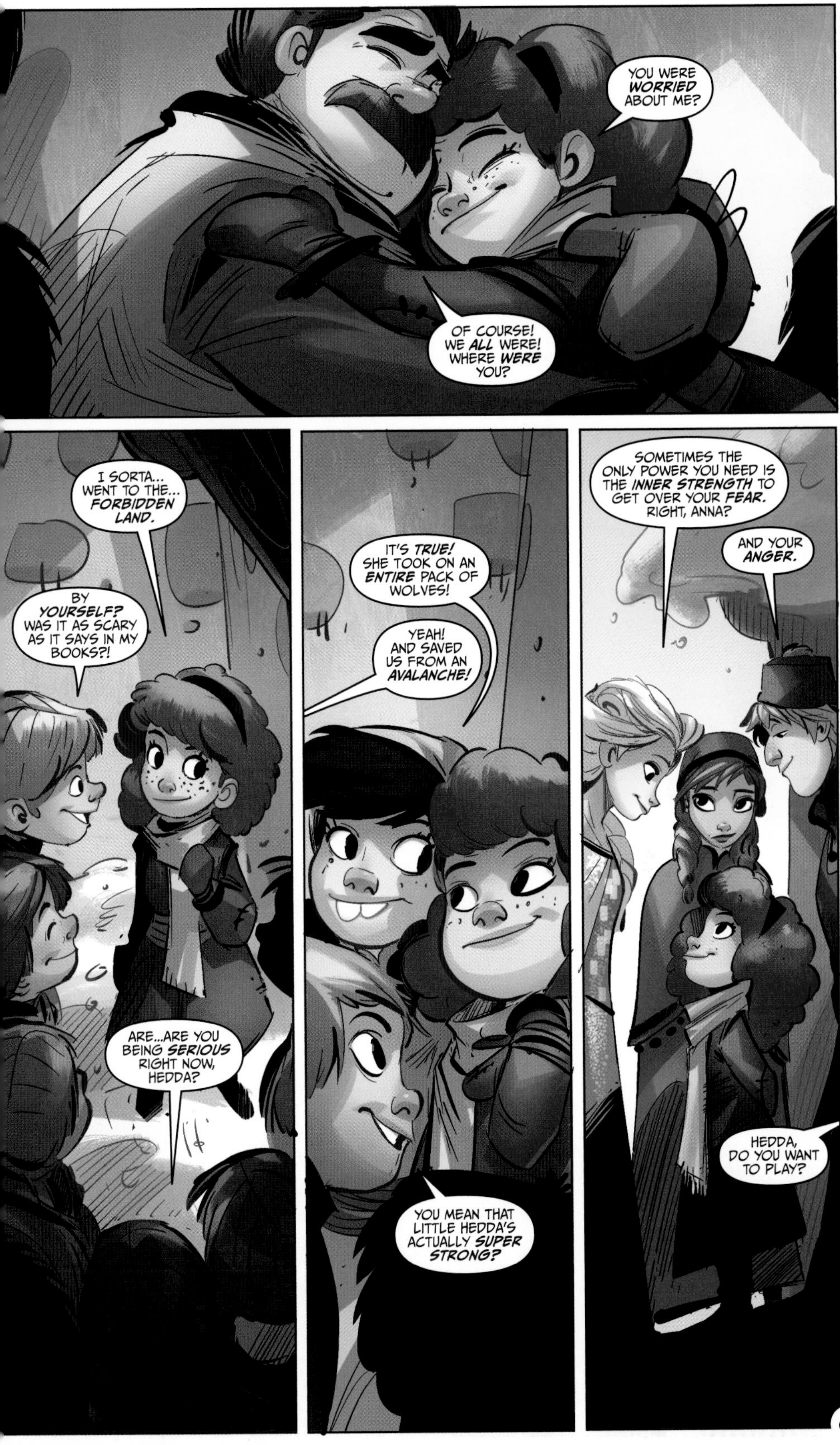

YOU WERE *WORRIED* ABOUT ME?
OF COURSE! WE *ALL* WERE! WHERE *WERE* YOU?
I SORTA... WENT TO THE... *FORBIDDEN LAND.*
BY *YOURSELF?* WAS IT AS SCARY AS IT SAYS IN MY BOOKS?!
ARE...ARE YOU BEING *SERIOUS* RIGHT NOW, HEDDA?
IT'S *TRUE!* SHE TOOK ON AN *ENTIRE* PACK OF WOLVES!
YEAH! AND SAVED US FROM AN *AVALANCHE!*
YOU MEAN THAT LITTLE HEDDA'S ACTUALLY *SUPER STRONG?*
SOMETIMES THE ONLY POWER YOU NEED IS THE *INNER STRENGTH* TO GET OVER YOUR *FEAR.* RIGHT, ANNA?
AND YOUR *ANGER.*
HEDDA, DO YOU WANT TO PLAY?

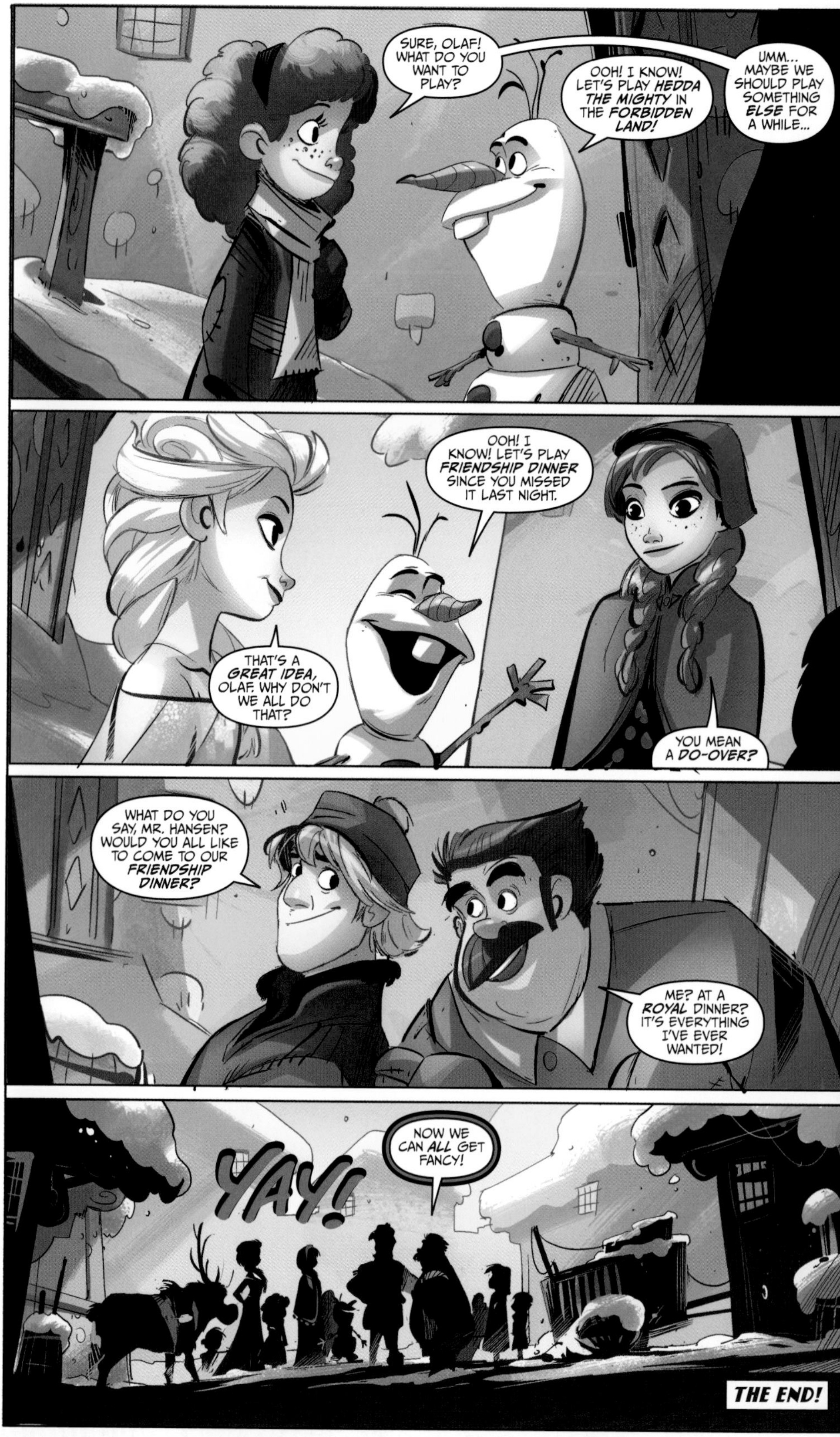
SURE, OLAF! WHAT DO YOU WANT TO PLAY?
OOH! I KNOW! LET'S PLAY HEDDA THE MIGHTY IN THE FORBIDDEN LAND!
UMM... MAYBE WE SHOULD PLAY SOMETHING ELSE FOR A WHILE...
OOH! I KNOW! LET'S PLAY FRIENDSHIP DINNER SINCE YOU MISSED IT LAST NIGHT.
THAT'S A GREAT IDEA, OLAF. WHY DON'T WE ALL DO THAT?
YOU MEAN A DO-OVER?
WHAT DO YOU SAY, MR. HANSEN? WOULD YOU ALL LIKE TO COME TO OUR FRIENDSHIP DINNER?
ME? AT A ROYAL DINNER? IT'S EVERYTHING I'VE EVER WANTED!
YAY!
NOW WE CAN ALL GET FANCY!
THE END!

Looking for Disney *Frozen?*

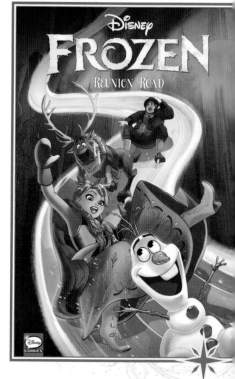

Disney Frozen
Breaking Boundaries

Anna is on a mission to find more ways that she can help the people of Arendelle. She makes a new friend and together they set out to explore the many jobs the kingdom has to offer! Meanwhile, Elsa is occupied with tension brewing in a nearby kingdom. Anna, Elsa, and friends have a quest to fulfill, mysteries to solve, and peace to restore!

978-1-50671-051-8 ❊ $10.99

Disney Frozen
Reunion Road

Elsa and Anna are invited to a harvest festival the kingdom of Snoob! When they discover th Kai has a long-lost brother there, they are set c a journey to reunite the two brothers. Along th way, they encounter dangerous mountain bridge wild animals, and runaway wagons, but als helpful new friends!

978-1-50671-270-3 ❊ $10.99

AVAILABLE AT YOUR LOCAL COMICS SHOP OR BOOKSTORE! TO FIND A COMICS SHOP IN YOUR AREA, VISIT COMICSHOPLOCATOR.COM

For more information or to order direct: On the web: DarkHorse.com | Email: mailorder@darkhorse.com
Phone: 1-800-862-0052 Mon.–Fri. 9 a.m. to 5 p.m. Pacific Time

Copyright © 2019 Disney Enterprises, Inc. Dark Horse Books® and the Dark Horse logo are registered trademarks of Dark Horse Comics LLC. All rights reserved. (BL8021)

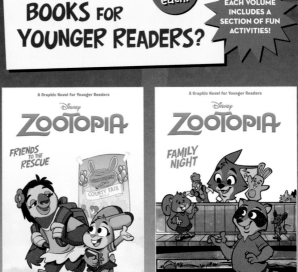

LOOKING FOR BOOKS FOR YOUNGER READERS?

$7.99 each!

EACH VOLUME INCLUDES A SECTION OF FUN ACTIVITIES!

Disney · PIXAR
INCREDIBLES 2
Heroes at Home
Disney COMICS

A Graphic Novel for Younger Readers
Disney
ZOOTOPIA
FRIENDS TO THE RESCUE
COUNTY FAIR
Disney COMICS

A Graphic Novel for Younger Readers
Disney
ZOOTOPIA
FAMILY NIGHT
Disney COMICS

A Graphic Novel for Younger Readers
Disney
PRINCESS
Jasmine's New Pet
Disney COMICS

A Graphic Novel for Younger Readers
Disney
PRINCESS
Ariel and the Sea Wolf
Disney COMICS

DISNEY ZOOTOPIA: FRIENDS TO THE RESCUE
ISBN 978-1-50671-054-9

DISNEY ZOOTOPIA: FAMILY NIGHT
ISBN 978-1-50671-053-2

Join young Judy Hopps as she uses wit and bravery to solve mysteries, conundrums, and more! And quick-thinking young Nick Wilde won't be stopped from achieving his goals—where there's a will, there's a way!

DISNEY·PIXAR INCREDIBLES 2: HEROES AT HOME
ISBN 978-1-50670-943-7

Being part of a Super family means helping out at home, too. Can Violet and Dash pick up groceries and secretly stop some bad guys? And can they clean up the house while Jack-Jack is "sleeping"?

DISNEY PRINCESS: JASMINE'S NEW PET
ISBN 978-1-50671-052-5

Jasmine has a new pet tiger, Rajah, but he's not quite ready for palace life. Will she be able to train the young cub before the Sultan finds him another home?

DISNEY PRINCESS: ARIEL AND THE SEA WOLF
ISBN 978-1-50671-203-1

Ariel accidentally drops a bracelet into a cave that supposedly contains a dangerous creature. Her curiosity implores her to enter, and what she finds turns her quest for a bracelet into a quest for truth.

AVAILABLE AT YOUR LOCAL COMICS SHOP OR BOOKSTORE! TO FIND A COMICS SHOP IN YOUR AREA, VISIT COMICSHOPLOCATOR.COM

For more information or to order direct: On the web: DarkHorse.com | Email: mailorder@darkhorse.com
Phone: 1-800-862-0052 Mon.–Fri. 9 a.m. to 5 p.m. Pacific Time

Disney

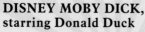

CLASSIC STORIES RETOLD
WITH THE MAGIC OF DISNEY!

Disney
TREASURE ISLAND
STARRING MICKEY MOUSE

DISNEY TREASURE ISLAND, starring Mickey Mouse

Robert Louis Stevenson's classic tale of pirates, treasure, and swashbuckling adventure comes to life in this adaptation!

978-1-50671-158-4 ✠ $10.99

Disney
Don·Quixote
STARRING Goofy AND Mickey Mouse

DISNEY DON QUIXOTE, starring Goofy & Mickey Mouse

A knight-errant and the power of his imagination finds reality in this adaptation of the classic by Miguel de Cervantes!

978-1-50671-216-1 ✠ $10.99

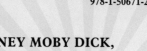

Disney
MOBY DICK
STARRING
Donald Duck

DISNEY MOBY DICK, starring Donald Duck

In an adaptation of Herman Melville's classic, sailors venture out on the high seas in pursuit of the white whale Moby Dick.

978-1-50671-157-7 ✠ $10.99

Disney
Dracula
STARRING MICKEY MOUSE

DISNEY DRACULA, starring Mickey Mouse

Enter a world where vampires rise up from the shadows in this adaptation of Bram Stoker's classic horror!

978-1-50671-217-8 ✠ $10.99

Disney
HAMLET
STARRING DONALD DUCK

DISNEY HAMLET, starring Donald Duck

The ghost of a betrayed king appoints Prince Ducklet to restore peace to his kingdom in this adaptation of William Shakespeare's tragedy.

978-1-50671-219-2 ✠ $10.99

Disney
FRANKENSTEIN
STARRING DONALD DUCK

DISNEY FRANKENSTEIN, starring Donald Duck

An electrifying adaptation of the classic novel by Mary Shelley exploring themes of nature and fate!

978-1-50671-218-5 ✠ $10.99

DARK HORSE BOOKS

AVAILABLE AT YOUR LOCAL COMICS SHOP OR BOOKSTORE! To find a comics shop in your area, visit comicshoplocator.com. For more information or to order direct: ✠ On the web: DarkHorse.com ✠ Email: mailorder@darkhorse.com ✠ Phone: 1-800-862-0052 Mon.–Fri. 9 a.m. to 5 p.m. Pacific Time

Disney COMICS

CATCH UP WITH DISNEY·PIXAR'S INCREDIBLES 2!

DISNEY·PIXAR INCREDIBLES 2
CRISIS IN MID-LIFE! & OTHER STORIES

An encounter with villain Bomb Voyage inspires Bob to begin training the next generation of Supers, Dash and Violet. Mr. Incredible will find himself needing to pull his family back together . . . because Bomb Voyage is still at large! In another story, Bob tells the kids about a battle from his glory days that seems too amazing to be true—but they never imagined the details would include their mom and dad's super secret first date . . . Finally, in two adventures all his own, baby Jack-Jack and his powers are set to save the day.

978-1-50671-019-8 • $10.99

DISNEY·PIXAR INCREDIBLES 2
SECRET IDENTITIES

It's tough being a teenager, and on top of that, a teenager with powers! Violet feels out of place at school and doesn't fit in with the kids around her . . . until she meets another girl at school—an outsider with powers, just like her! But when her new friend asks her to keep a secret, Violet is torn between keeping her word and doing what's right.

978-1-50671-392-2 • $10.99

AVAILABLE AT YOUR LOCAL COMICS SHOP OR BOOKSTORE! TO FIND A COMICS SHOP IN YOUR AREA, VISIT COMICSHOPLOCATOR.COM

FOR MORE INFORMATION OR TO ORDER DIRECT: ON THE WEB: DARKHORSE.COM • EMAIL: MAILORDER@DARKHORSE.COM • PHONE: 1-800-862-0052 MON.–FRI. 9 AM TO 5 PM PACIFIC TIME

COPYRIGHT © 2019 DISNEY ENTERPRISES, INC. AND PIXAR. DARK HORSE BOOKS® AND THE DARK HORSE LOGO ARE REGISTERED TRADEMARKS OF DARK HORSE COMICS LLC. ALL RIGHTS RESERVED. (BL8022)

DARK HORSE BOOKS

CATCH UP WITH WOODY AND FRIENDS FROM DISNEY·PIXAR'S *TOY STORY*!

Disney·Pixar Toy Story: Adventures

A collection of short comic stories based on the animated films Disney·Pixar *Toy Story*, *Toy Story 2*, and *Toy Story 3*!

Set your jets for adventure. Join Woody, Buzz, and all of your *Toy Story* favorites in a variety of fun and exciting comic stories. Get ready to play with your favorite toys with Andy and Bonnie, join the toys as they take more journeys to the outside, play make-believe in a world of infinite possibilities, meet new friends, and have a party or two—experience all of this and more!

Volume 1 | 978-1-50671-266-6 | $10.99
Volume 2 | 978-1-50671-451-6 | $10.99

Disney·Pixar Toy Story 4

A graphic novel anthology expanding on the animated blockbuster Disney·Pixar *Toy Story 4*.

Join Woody and the *Toy Story* gang in four connecting stories set before and after Disney·Pixar's *Toy Story 4*.

978-1-50671-265-9 | $10.99

AVAILABLE AT YOUR LOCAL COMICS SHOP OR BOOKSTORE!
To find a comics shop in your area, visit **comicshoplocator.com** For more information or to order direct: On the web: **DarkHorse.com** Email: **mailorder@darkhorse.com** Phone: **1-800-862-0052** Mon.–Fri. 9 a.m. to 5 p.m. Pacific Time

Copyright © 2019 Disney Enterprises, Inc. and Pixar. Dark Horse Books® and the Dark Horse logo are registered trademarks of Dark Horse Comics LLC. All rights reserved. (BL8016)